FIRE FROM HEAVEN

Fire from Heaven

16

LEFT BEHIND

>THE KIDS<

Jerry B. Jenkins

Tim LaHaye

WITH CHRIS FABRY

TYNDALE
KIDS

TYNDALE HOUSE PUBLISHERS, INC.
WHEATON, ILLINOIS

Visit Tyndale's exciting Web site at www.tyndale.com

Discover the latest Left Behind news at www.leftbehind.com

Published in association with the literary agency of Alive Communications, Inc., 7680 Goddard Street, Suite 200, Colorado Springs, CO 80920.

Scripture quotations are taken from the *Holy Bible,* New Living Translation, copyright © 1996. Used by permission of Tyndale House Publishers, Inc., Wheaton, Illinois 60189. All rights reserved.

Scripture taken from the New King James Version. Copyright © 1979, 1980, 1982 by Thomas Nelson, Inc. Used by permission. All rights reserved.

Edited by Curtis H. C. Lundgren

ISBN 0-8423-4297-4

Printed in the United States of America

08   07   06   05   04   03   02   01

9   8   7   6   5   4   3   2   1

To Crystal, Tiffany, William, and Stephen

TABLE OF CONTENTS

What's Gone On Before

JUDD Thompson Jr. and the rest of the Young Tribulation Force are involved in an intense struggle. The Global Community noose is tightening.

Lionel Washington helps Vicki escape, and they join the others at a secret cave near the Stahley mansion. The kids have close calls with Global Community guards, but they gather supplies to stay alive.

After hearing of the possible execution of their friend Mr. Stein, Judd sets up a meeting with Commander Blancka. With the help of biker Pete and his friends, Judd, Lionel, and Vicki confront the commander and his troops. Taylor Graham, previously thought to be dead, steals a GC helicopter and fires at GC troops.

With skies darkening, the kids speed away. As GC snipers set their sights on them, the skies open. Hail falls and the kids scramble to safety. Judd and the others realize this is another judgment of God as the hail turns to fire and blood.

The Young Trib Force meets a safe distance from Chicago. Mark's cousin, John Preston, reaches them by E-mail, then talks with Judd and Mark by phone. The Global Community Navy has forced John into service. John is assigned a communications post on the *Peacekeeper 1*, a ship headed out to the Atlantic Ocean.

The kids know the dangers ahead, but they determine to follow God and fight the enemies of their souls, no matter the cost.

ONE

John's Message

JOHN Preston sat at the communications
center of the United North American States
ship *Peacekeeper 1*, wondering if he would
ever see his friends again. Less than two years
earlier, he and his cousin Mark Eisman had
met Judd Thompson Jr. on their first day
back at Nicolae High. The kids had seen their
share of trouble, and even death. Several
times John had begun typing a message but
erased it when someone came near. He had
to wait for the right moment.

John had hoped the kids could be together
at the Meeting of the Witnesses in Jerusalem.
Now that seemed out of the question. John
had set up a computer in his quarters to
record each session and couldn't wait to hear
Tsion Ben-Judah teach live.

An alarm sent people scurrying. Officers

barked orders. John studied a blip on a radar screen and pointed it out to his friend, Carl.

Carl nodded. "Finally gonna see some action."

After the Wrath of the Lamb earthquake, John had been taken from college and put to work with the Global Community Navy. Carl had taken John under his wing. There didn't seem to be anything about computers or technical equipment Carl didn't understand.

Carl smiled. "Only ships allowed out here now are GC approved," he said.

"Who else would want to be?"

"Drug pushers, weapons dealers, you name it," Carl said. "We consider them modern-day pirates."

"Three miles and closing, sir," an officer shouted.

"Should we be worried, Carl?"

Carl smiled. "Not even God could sink *Peacekeeper 1*. Best communications, most precise weaponry, and amazing speed."

John stared through a scope at what looked like a cargo ship.

"No registry evident, sir," an officer reported.

Carl raised his eyebrows. "Guys on deck," he said.

John saw patrols with high-powered rifles walking back and forth.

"Attention," the captain said over the loud-speaker. "The ship we're intersecting is in violation of Global Community maritime law. We could destroy it from here, but we suspect illegal weapons and hostages."

Carl shook his head. "I don't like their chances."

"We're sending a team into the water before the ship spots us," the captain contin-ued. "We'll give the hostages every chance."

John watched the undersea monitor. *Peace-keeper 1*'s small sub approached the cargo ship, and men in wet suits floated through the hatch. Another monitor displayed a few climbing the side of the ship.

The captain rushed to the communications center and pushed the talk button in front of John. "Stay down! Stay down! Unfriendlies coming your way."

But they had been spotted. The men in wet suits dropped back into the water as men onboard opened fire. John saw blood in the water. One diver made it back to the sub.

The captain ordered pursuit, and the sudden acceleration threw John back in his chair. The cargo ship turned to flee, but it was no match for *Peacekeeper 1*.

"They don't stand a chance," Carl said.

"What about the hostages?" John said.

Carl shook his head.

As they closed in, bullets pinged off the hull, and John saw the frightened faces of the enemy patrols.

"Warning," the captain said over the loudspeaker. "Release your hostages now or we sink your ship."

The patrols fled below deck. John thought they might release hostages, but two masked men returned with bazookas. John felt the explosion, and the captain rattled off a series of orders. The *Peacekeeper 1* turned its guns on the scared crew.

Carl shook his head. "Idiots," he said.

Peacekeeper 1's cannon opened a huge hole in the cargo ship. It tipped one way, then the other. As water filled the hole, the crew leaped overboard. John saw one of the divers from the *Peacekeeper 1* scramble onto the deck of the other ship and disappear into a smoke-filled stairwell.

"Pelton, no!" the captain shouted. "Get him out of there!"

Carl clicked a button and spoke to the diver, but there was no response.

John's heart raced as five civilians appeared through the smoke. As soon as they hit the sloping deck, they slipped and fell over the railing. Within seconds the submarine surfaced and picked two civilians from the water. John watched for any sign of the diver who had performed the rescue. Just as the stairwell sank below the waterline, the diver emerged. The submarine surfaced. John moved closer to the monitors.

Seconds seemed like an eternity. A whoop went up in the ship as the lone diver shot out of the water with the three remaining civilians clinging to him.

Since the judgment of fire, hail, and blood, the kids had hidden at the gas station. Judd was surprised by the anger of the Young Trib Force.

Shelly began, "We've been—"

"I don't want to hear her," Mark said. "She turned and ran."

"What are you talking about?" Shelly said.

"You took the easy way out and got a ride without facing Blancka," Mark said.

Vicki's face flushed. "You have no right to judge," she said. "You don't know what she's been through."

"We've all been through a lot," Mark said. "Let's not decide stuff on emotion."

Shelly's lip trembled. Judd cut in. "Everybody is equal," he said. "We'll listen to every-body."

Vicki crossed her arms. "He probably wants to go blow people up, like Taylor Graham."

"If it weren't for Taylor," Mark said, "we'd have never gotten out of there. Judd's plan was wimpy."

"Everybody be quiet!" Judd yelled. Judd saw Taylor storm out the front of the gas station.

Conrad put his face in his hands. "I didn't know it was gonna be like this."

Judd closed the office door. Boyd Walker, manager of the gas station, and Judd's friend Pete stood nearby.

Shelly stood up. "That's it. Either Mark goes or I do."

Mr. Stein stepped forward. "I am new to this," he said. "We have been through a lot. We could have died yesterday."

"Not her," Mark said.

"From what I understand," Mr. Stein said, "this young woman intervened on your behalf at the Stahley mansion."

"Yeah," Vicki said.

Mr. Stein put up a hand and stared at Mark. "Is it not true she put her life on the line and could have been arrested by the Global Community guards, not once, but twice?"

"I'm not saying she can't be part of the group," Mark stammered, "I just—"

"I have read only a little of the Scriptures, but aren't we supposed to love each other?" Mr. Stein sat. Everyone seemed a little calmer. Judd nodded at Lionel.

"Tsion's E-mail got to me," Lionel said. "With all the judgments coming, we don't know how much longer we have left. We have to be smart but bold."

"What does that mean?" Vicki said.

"People need to know the truth," Lionel said. "If we hide, we're wasting a chance to be part of the soul harvest."

Judd said, "The Global Community knows our faces. We're spending our energy running from them."

"Shelly, Mark, and John are the only ones they're not onto," Lionel said.

Darrion spoke up. "My family has a place in Wisconsin," she said. "If it survived the earthquake, we could go there."

"I'm tired of running," Vicki said.

The meeting ended. The kids argued every day. Mr. Stein pestered Judd for Tsion Ben-Judah's private E-mail address, but Judd was reluctant. Tsion was busy and Judd didn't want to bother him. But Judd had finally relented, and Tsion had written to Mr.

Stein. The rabbi encouraged him to get to Israel, but recommended against a face-to-face meeting in the States.

Mr. Stein said he had hidden a stash of money before he was arrested by the Global Community. In the wee hours of the morning, Mr. Stein, Taylor Graham, and Judd's friend Pete prepared to retrieve the money. Judd awoke and heard the rumble of motorcycles.

Pete stuck his head in the door. "Looks like we've got company. Hide."

Judd recognized the voice of Red, the big, long-haired biker with an attitude. "Guess you're pretty proud of yourself for breaking up the gang," Red said.

"We didn't have to split," Pete said. "You decided to leave."

Red cursed. "The holy rollers in there?" he said.

"If you mean the rest of the gang, no," Pete said. "They moved on. You want to come inside?"

"Done talkin'," Red said.

Judd saw a light in the window of the gas station. He ducked but it was too late. A bearded man with two gold teeth looked at him. "Gotcha," Gold Tooth said. "Hey, Red," the man shouted as he ran to the front. "Think we got something back there!"

Before his shift began, John stood on deck and watched the sun rise over the ocean. He had grown up singing about God's love being as wide as the sea, but he had never seen anything so impressive.

Carl approached, clutching a piece of paper.

"I was thinking about those kidnappers," John said. "You think the sharks—"

"Look," Carl interrupted. He handed John a fax. It looked like a drawing of something in space.

John shook his head. "I don't get it."

"You will," Carl said. "It's a new meteor."

John rolled his eyes. "Big deal."

"It *is* a big deal," Carl said. "This thing's headed straight for Earth."

John remembered Tsion Ben-Judah's warning about an object falling from the sky. A judgment from God. He studied the picture closely.

"When's it supposed to hit?" John said.

TWO

The Comet

JUDD hurried to the front of the gas station. The guy with the gold teeth ran to Red.

"I thought you were smarter than that," Judd heard Red say. "I know who's back there."

"God's trying to get your attention," Pete said.

Red pulled a crumpled piece of paper from his back pocket. "And the Global Community's gonna get yours," he said. "There's a GC post about a half hour from here."

Pete looked toward the station and frowned. Judd knew what was on the paper.

"Don't do this," Pete said.

"Watch me," Red said as he kicked his motorcycle to a start and sped off. The gold-toothed man followed.

Pete ran a hand through his hair and walked into the station. He handed Judd the paper. Mug shots of Vicki, Lionel, Conrad, Darrion, and Judd. Also a description of Mr. Stein. "Reward for information leading to an arrest and conviction."

The others slowly filed into the room.

"Think he'll turn us in?" Vicki said.

Pete shook his head. "Can't take the chance," he said. He put on his helmet and started his motorcycle. "If I'm not back in an hour, get out of here."

"You can't go up against all of them," Lionel protested.

"I won't let Red do this to you," Pete said. He throttled and roared off.

Boyd Walker leaned quietly against an old soda machine. "I have an idea if you're interested," he said. "A fellow in Des Plaines owns a gas station a lot like this one. His son has a little business on the side—tattoos. He might help you."

"I don't understand," Judd said.

"Kid's a genius," the man said. "Phony IDs and disguises."

"New identities?" Lionel said.

"I can't see us going anywhere near there," Vicki said.

"Zeke and Zeke Jr.," the manager said, writing it down.

Shelly stepped forward. "We need to do something now." She found a pair of scissors and some hair coloring for sale on a dusty shelf. Vicki's hair went from strawberry red to jet black and shorter than ever. Judd was almost bald when Shelly was through with him. The kids stood in a line.

"Not bad," Mark said. "Now all you guys need are some fake IDs."

The phone rang. The manager handed it to Mark.

"John?" Mark said.

Judd and Vicki gathered around. Mark said a few words, then put the phone down.

"What did he say?" Judd said.

"Told me there wasn't time to talk," Mark said. "Didn't want them catching him making the call. He said to turn on the television and watch. Then he said it was going to be some ride."

Judd flicked on the television. News bulletins interrupted every station.

Newscasters reported that only a few hours ago astronomers had discovered a brand-new comet on a collision course with Earth. The Global Community Aeronautics and Space Administration (GCASA) had probes circling the object. The data they sent back was startling.

"Under normal conditions," a spokesman for GCASA said, "we would have seen this a few months or even a few years ago. But these aren't normal conditions. I can't explain why we just located it today."

"Doctor, this meteor is how far from us right now?" the male anchor said.

"*Meteor* is the wrong term," the scientist said. "You were correct when you called it a comet. The data shows the comet to have a consistency of sandstone. Very brittle. When it enters Earth's atmosphere, it should disintegrate."

"Should?"

"It's impossible that it will miss us, unless it can be destroyed before it enters the atmosphere."

"And when will that happen?" the anchor said.

The scientist squirmed. "I'd rather let our director address that when he gives an update."

Judd moved closer to the television as a picture from the probe flashed on the screen. "Look at the size of that thing."

"What else have you learned?" the anchor said.

"The comet is irregularly shaped, but it's immense. Global Community astronomers estimate it is no less than the mass of the entire Appalachian Mountain range."

"Wow!" Lionel said. "How could they not see that until this morning?"

The anchor furrowed his brow. "And what kind of damage could something that big actually do?"

"The potential is enormous," the scientist said. "On a scale of one to ten, ten being the worst, I'd say this is a . . . ten and a half."

"We're all gonna die!" Shelly said.

Judd turned.

"W-w-we studied this in school," she stammered.

Vicki hugged Shelly. "It's gonna be okay."

"That's not gonna happen," Judd said.

"Let's say it is as hard as granite," the anchor said. "What then?"

"Once the object comes into Earth's gravitational pull, it will accelerate to thirty-two feet per second squared. No matter what it is made of, it will burst into flames. Pieces will fall to Earth."

"Worst case, what could happen?"

The scientist stared at the camera. "Worst case? Earth would be split in two."

The news anchor sat speechless.

The scientist added, "Or our orbit could be altered. Either would be disastrous for the planet."

"We're gonna die," a biker said.

Someone handed the anchor a piece of paper from off camera. "This message from

GCASA," he said, stunned. "The . . . uh . . . collision will occur at approximately 6 P.M. New Babylon time, which is midnight in Tokyo, 3 P.M. in London, and 10 A.M. New York time."

"Nine our time," Vicki said.

"It's seven now," Lionel said.

In his quarters, John pulled out his Bible and turned to Revelation. He remembered something Tsion Ben-Judah had said about a meteor.

John found the passage that talked about the hail they had just come through. The next verse said, "Then the second angel blew his trumpet, and a great mountain of fire was thrown into the sea. And one-third of the water in the sea became blood. And one-third of all things living in the sea died. And one-third of all the ships on the sea were destroyed."

The verses sent a chill through him. *The comet is coming from God. It will fall somewhere over the water. But where?*

John pulled up the rabbi's Web site and found a message concerning the disaster.

This is the second Trumpet Judgment foretold in Revelation 8:8-9. Will we

look like experts when the results are
in? Will it shock the powers-that-be to
discover that, just as the Bible says,
one-third of the fish will die and
one-third of the ships at sea will sink,
and tidal waves will wreak havoc on the
entire world? Or will officials reinterpret
the event to make it appear the Bible
was wrong? Do not be fooled! Do not
delay! Now is the accepted time. Now is
the day of salvation. Come to Christ
before it is too late. Things will only get
worse. We were all left behind the first
time. Do not be left wanting when you
breathe your last.

John put his head in his hands. He thought
of Carl. He hadn't talked with him about
God. *Maybe it isn't too late.*

He quickly typed a message to the rest of
the Young Trib Force and sent it. He ran to
the command center and found Carl amid
a whirl of activity.

"I have to talk to you," John said.

"Things are nuts right now," Carl said.
"They're talking about shooting the thing
down before it hits." Carl handed John a
printout. "It's going to hit here in the Atlantic. They say it's the best possible scenario."

"Best for who?" John said. The Global

Community predicted tidal waves would engulf coasts on both sides of the Atlantic for up to fifty miles inland. Coastal areas had already begun evacuating.

"If they don't shoot the thing down there's no way we'll survive," Carl said.

John looked at a monitor and saw a simulation of the impact. An incredible wall of water stretched to the sky. Carl was right. No way anyone could survive.

Vicki was relieved when the news anchor reported the comet was heading for the Atlantic. She drew close to the screen. The earthquake had killed so many people, but it came without warning. This was worse.

"Those military personnel and passengers and crew members on other oceangoing vessels that can be reached in time are being airlifted to safety."

"John!" Vicki said. "He was headed to the Atlantic, wasn't he?"

Judd nodded and looked around the room for Mark.

"I'll get him," Vicki said.

Vicki found Mark outside, staring at the sky. She explained the situation, and Mark's shoulders slumped.

"We've been through so much," Mark said.

Vicki left Mark. She found Judd intently watching the coverage. An anchorman put a hand to his ear and nodded. "We're being told now that His Excellency, Potentate Nicolae Carpathia, is prepared to address this crisis. We go now to the Global Community Headquarters in New Babylon."

Nicolae spoke from his plush office. "My brothers and sisters in the Global Community, we have weathered many storms together, and it appears there is another on the horizon. Let me first answer a question that has come up, and that is, How could we not have known?

"I assure you, our personnel alerted us to this potential disaster as quickly as possible. We could not have known about this phenomenon any earlier.

"I am also confident, having taken precautions with my military advisors some time ago, that we have the firepower to destroy this object. However, we have been advised that an attempt to destroy the comet would be too great a risk to life on our planet. We cannot predict where the fragments might fall. The risk is simply unacceptable, especially considering that this falling mountain is on course to land in the ocean.

"We will keep you informed of any developments as we know them. Please cooperate with the officials in your area. We will get through this difficult time together, as we build a stronger world."

The crew of the *Peacekeeper 1* assembled on deck. They stood at attention as the captain explained the situation. The men looked shell-shocked.

"I had hoped to have better news," the captain said. "Potentate Carpathia has decided not to try and shoot the comet down."

The crew groaned in unison.

The captain held up a hand. "We're heading away from the impact point as fast as we can, but if the scientists are correct, there's no way we'll outrun the thing.

"There is one chance," the captain continued. "We've recovered the submarine. If we get far enough away from impact and the sub goes down far enough, some may be able to survive."

"That thing can hold only a handful of people," John whispered to Carl.

"We'll draw names within the hour," the captain said.

THREE

The Sacrifice

JUDD watched for Pete while the kids searched for the latest about the comet. Finally, Pete rolled in. He did a double take at Judd and the others.

"What happened?" Judd said.

Pete shook his head. "Don't want to talk about it. Let's just say you're safe for the time being."

The group gathered around the television. Updated pictures from the probes showed the comet in more detail. It was light in color. The anchorman reported, "Ladies and gentlemen, I urge you to put this in perspective. This object is about to enter Earth's atmosphere. It should burst into flames any second."

Lionel called Judd to the laptop and showed him what Tsion Ben-Judah had written. Judd ran a hand over his head. "I sure hope John's not near that thing."

The coverage switched to a local reporter. The man's voice sounded urgent. "GCASA projects the collision at approximately 9:00 A.M. Chicago time. If the predictions are accurate, the collision will take place in the middle of the Atlantic Ocean. But keep in mind that if the comet splits, fragments could possibly fall in the Midwest."

"Splashdown is less than an hour away," Vicki said.

The reporter continued, "I'm told by one meteorologist that this kind of disruption could cause severe weather around the globe. We won't deal with tidal waves like the coastal areas, but we may see strong winds and possibly tornadoes."

The crew stood silently watching as the captain picked the remaining names to occupy the sub. The rescued hostages were given priority. That left only seven seats for the crew.

John looked at Carl. "I don't like these odds," Carl said.

The sixth name the captain called was John's. Carl patted him on the shoulder.

John sighed heavily and nearly fell to his knees. But he couldn't shake the truth. He hadn't given the most important message to his friends.

"You're the lucky one," Carl said, shaking hands.

"I need to talk with you," John said. "Now."

When the last name was called, John took Carl to his room and opened his Bible. "I haven't talked to anybody on the ship about this. I was scared to."

John quickly explained the plan of salvation. He told Carl everyone has sinned. "Everyone is separated from God. Jesus died to bring us back to God. People who ask forgiveness in Jesus' name will spend eternity in heaven."

Carl shook his head. "Staring at death makes you think. I figure God will accept me for the good stuff I've done. If not, saying a prayer won't help."

"It's not like that," John said. "God can't accept anything that's less than perfect. That's why Jesus came. He lived a perfect life—"

"Preston!" the captain shouted. "If you want to get off this ship, you go now."

John looked at Carl. Carl shrugged. "Sorry, I can't buy it."

"Preston, now!" the captain said.

"Sir," John said, "I'd like to give my spot to Carl."

The captain furrowed his brow. "Don't be foolish, son. This is your chance to survive."

John opened his Bible. He scribbled something inside the cover. "Read this later. I want to do this. I have some friends who can help you. If you make it back, look them up and tell them what happened."

Carl staggered. "You can't do this, man. You hardly even know me."

"I know what I'm doing," John said. "Read this stuff. It'll change your life if you let it."

The captain scowled at John and took Carl away. John took a deep breath as Carl squeezed into the sub. The crew stood on deck and watched as the sub slipped beneath the surface and headed to the bottom of the ocean.

"I don't know why you did that," the captain said when he returned to John.

"I'd like to speak with the others," John said, "before splashdown."

The captain shook his head. "I'd like to let you, Preston," he said. "After what you did today, you deserve it. But it's against policy."

"Sir, with all due respect, we're gonna die in less than an hour. I have something to say that could change everything. For you and the others."

"Sorry, Preston," the captain said. He walked away.

Vicki felt nervous about the comet. Even though it was supposed to land in the ocean, part of her felt they were still in danger. The way Pete acted when he returned spooked her as well.

As the moments ticked down, the kids watched the updates. A disabled cruise ship was stranded in the Atlantic.

Shelly put a hand to her mouth. "Those poor people," she said.

"Other Global Community vessels are at sea," the reporter continued, "but rescue operations are impossible with the splash-down so close. Efforts to move boats to safety along the Atlantic shoreline have stopped."

There were reports of some who refused to evacuate their homes. "Stayin' right here," a grizzled old man said. "Lived through the disappearances and the earthquake. Don't see any reason why I can't live through a big wave."

Vicki looked at Judd. She had been so

angry and hurt by him. But the possibility of losing their lives put things in perspective. Their fights seemed petty compared to the fact that a comet could split the earth in two and send them hurtling into space. She believed that wouldn't happen because of what the Bible said, but the prospect made her shudder.

Vicki thought about Phoenix and her promise to Ryan. She longed to find the dog, not only to keep her word, but also because the dog reminded her of Ryan. Phoenix had helped Ryan move through the pain of losing his parents. Vicki thought the dog could do the same for her.

After the launch of the sub, John and the rest of the crew were in a daze. They were trapped. Moving to any part of the ship was pointless. They were about to see a wave unlike any in the history of the world.

John knew his decision to let Carl have his spot would be considered heroic by some and foolish by others. He didn't feel like a hero. He was sorry that he hadn't told the others about Christ.

John looked at the empty command center and thought, *What have I got to lose?*

He hurried to the command center and punched the controls that sealed both entrances. He flipped the switch that let him speak to the entire ship and pecked on the microphone.

"Test . . . can you hear me?" John said.

The captain and a few officers came running. When they tried to open the door, John put up a hand. He prayed silently, his hands shaking. Then he keyed the microphone.

"My name is John Preston. The captain wouldn't let me talk to you, so I've had to sorta take over. I don't mean any harm by this, and I promise to open the doors in just a minute. First, I want you to hear me out."

The captain beat on the door. John couldn't hear the man's voice, but he could read his lips. "This is mutiny," he said. John turned his back and knelt under a desk.

"My name was chosen to go in the sub, but I let a friend take my place. I couldn't go and not tell you guys about living forever."

John peered through the transparent but bulletproof glass and saw the entire crew standing on deck. Some looked toward the command center. Others turned and walked away. John heard pounding behind him and kept talking.

"When I was a kid, my parents used to take me to church. I sang and did my time in Sunday school. But it didn't sink in. I never really thought what I was singing about was true.

"Then came the disappearances, and most of my family was taken away. I wished I'd listened closer. Maybe some of you lost friends and family too.

"When the captain called my name, I was relieved to have a chance to survive. But the more I thought, the more I knew I had to stay. I want to tell you about the person who can save you."

John didn't hear pounding and wondered whether the captain was listening or figuring out a way to get in.

"The comet is a judgment from God. It's meant to get your attention. It's predicted in the Bible. Everything the Bible says has come true.

"Unless a miracle happens, we're gonna die. Each one of us will stand before a holy God. If you've done anything wrong, *anything*, God will have to turn you away."

John looked out over the crew. Several stood with their arms crossed, listening intently. Others milled about and laughed nervously. John turned. The captain had a gun. Someone was talking with him. *The diver who had saved the hostages!*

"Everybody's done wrong things," John said. "Everybody deserves to be turned away. But God loved us enough to put himself on the line and give his life. Jesus was God. He lived a perfect life and died in your place, in my place."

A burst of light flashed. John heard a boom that shook the window. The crew hit the deck.

"We don't have much time," John screamed. "If you ask Jesus to forgive you, he will. And when you're in front of God, he won't see the bad things you've done. He'll see the perfect life of Jesus."

Some of the men talked to each other. Several cried and looked toward the sky. The captain stared at John, his hands against the glass.

An eerie silence fell over the gas station as Judd and the others watched. As the news anchor talked, he picked up a pen, then repeatedly pulled off its cap and put it back on.

"The Global Community military has positioned aircraft so we can see the first glimpse of this more than one-thousand-mile-square mountain as it enters our atmosphere," the anchor said.

A spokesman for the Global Community Aeronautics and Space Administration revealed a final report. The object consisted largely of sulfur. When the mountain broke through the atmosphere, Judd and the others heard a terrific boom. Windows in the station shattered.

"The comet has now entered our atmosphere and has burst into flames," the spokesman said. "The trajectory will take it into the Atlantic as expected." He paused. "The next few minutes should be spectacular."

The sky turned black as the comet eclipsed the sun. The burning ball of death was heading straight for them.

John turned on the outside microphone and listened as men cried out, "No! God help us!"

"You can be sure of heaven," John continued, trembling. "Pray with me. God, I'm sorry for the bad things I've done. I believe Jesus died for me. Come into my heart right now and forgive me."

Most of the men were still lying on the deck. A few knelt. John saw several with marks on their foreheads. "I'll meet those who want to talk more at the front of the ship," John said as he opened the doors.

The captain burst through with two guards. "Arrest him!"

The captain grabbed the microphone and yelled, "We're going to die like men! We don't need religion."

The crew panicked. A group rushed John and the guards who were holding him.

"Get him to the brig, now!" the captain yelled.

"What's going to happen to us?" a young man screamed.

Officers whisked John down the stairs before he could answer. They left him in a dank cell.

A few minutes passed. John wondered if he would die in this room. Then keys jangled and John saw the face of the diver who had rescued the hostages. The man turned slightly. In the dim light John saw the outline of the telltale mark on his forehead.

"You're being released into my custody," the man said.

"Why?" John said. "How?"

"Come on. There's not much time." He put out his hand. "I talked with the captain after you were taken away. I convinced him you could calm the crew down."

John followed the man on deck and walked to the front of the ship. The man held up a hand and asked for quiet. Clouds above them scrolled back. The wind picked up and the water became choppy. John held on as the ship bobbed on the surface like a child's toy. The man turned to John and nodded. "Go ahead. Say what you want."

John shouted over the noise, "Those of you who prayed, look at me. This mark on my forehead means I've been sealed by God. I'm his."

"I can see it," one man said.

"What mark are you talking about?" another said.

"If you can't see the mark," John said, "it means you don't believe." John went over the message again. A few prayed. Others had questions.

The sky took on a ghostly appearance. Black clouds rushed over the crew. The force of the comet was creating a weather phenomenon never experienced by anyone. Hurricane-force winds blew between the comet and the surface of the sea.

John looked at the men scurrying across the ship. He called together all who had the mark. "Go to everyone you can and tell them what happened to you. These guys need God. It's their last chance."

The men, shaking, spread out on the deck. Many of the crew ran to their quarters when they saw the darkening sky. One man wrestled a gun from a guard. He ran to the edge and raised the pistol. A shot rang out. His body fell into the surging water.

John bit his lip. *Just a few more minutes before it hits. It's hard to believe this is really happening.*

FOUR

Splashdown

MAYHEM. Confusion.

John had never seen anything like it. The sea churned. Men screamed and grabbed anything to keep from going over the edge.

The wind was furious. It nearly ripped John's clothes from his body. He fell to his hands and knees and crawled to the stairs leading to the command center.

"What are you doing?" the diver yelled behind him.

"I have to get a message to my cousin and his friends," John screamed.

"They'll throw you in the brig!" the diver said.

John turned. Huge waves washed over the bow. "I have to try."

Judd watched as experts paraded through the Global Community broadcasts. "What we're seeing may be a repeat of what happened millions of years ago with the dinosaurs," one scientist said.

"I still don't understand how this could sneak up on us," the anchor said.

"Funding for research has been small until the last few months," the scientist said. "Our best guess is that the comet was somehow thrown off course and came directly toward Earth."

The anchor took a deep breath. "I'm told we're about to see our first glimpse of the comet," he said.

Even on the small screen the sight made the kids gasp. The shot from the airplane showed a huge glowing mass heading for Earth. Gray and black clouds encircled the plane and the cameras lost sight of the comet for a moment.

Judd watched Mark fumble with the computer through tear-drenched eyes. "I just sent John a message," Mark said.

Judd put an arm around Mark.

"Five minutes until impact," the scientist said.

The captain threatened to throw John in the brig again, but the diver was able to talk him out of it. Several officers had been sick in the room. The smell turned John's stomach. As the crew in the command center grew frantic, John strapped himself in behind a computer and began typing.

One man urged the captain to turn the boat around. The captain shook his head. "No way we can outrun this. They're predicting tidal waves on both sides of the Atlantic. Where do we go?"

"We have to do something," the man said.

The captain looked at John and lowered his voice. "What you said before seemed to calm them. Can you do anything?"

John swiveled his chair toward the frightened men. Again he explained the gospel. The men listened. "God, you give a peace that passes our human understanding," John prayed. "I ask that you would help each of these men to know you now and that you would give them that peace."

"I've got a wife and a baby back at the base," a man interrupted. "What about them?"

John led the man in a prayer and told him

to quickly e-mail his wife and give her Tsion Ben-Judah's Web site. "She'll find out what to do by reading that."

Others left the room, but John was glad he had been given another chance. He opened an E-mail from Mark and read the hastily written message.

If you're where we think you are, Mark wrote, *you probably don't have time to read this. We all want you to know we're praying for you. You'll see Bruce and Ryan and Chaya before we will, so tell them we said hello.*

John finished reading through blurry eyes.

I know we've had our disagreements, and I haven't been the best cousin, Mark continued, *but I'm proud of you. I'll miss you.*

John put his head on the console and wept. He would never see Mark in this life again. Never talk with Judd or Vicki. If he'd gone in the submarine . . . but he couldn't think that way now. He recalled what Jesus said to his disciples: "The greatest love is shown when people lay down their lives for their friends."

"There it comes!" an officer shouted.

The others moved toward the window. John looked up.

Blinding light.

Clouds whirled.

Wave after wave tossed the ship.

John shielded his eyes. His skin, though exposed only a few seconds, turned red. John saw one man on deck put his hands over his eyes. The ship pitched and the man lost his balance, flipped, and tumbled into the railing. Like a rag doll, he went limp and fell over the edge.

John shook his head. The diver who had helped him came close. "Guess this is it," the man said.

"I can't remember your name," John said, extending a hand.

The man shook it firmly. "Jim Pelton."

"We'll have a lotta time to talk once this is over," John said, "when we're finally home."

"I don't like the thought of dying," Jim said. "I wanted to live until the glorious appearing of Christ. But I just realized, today I'll see members of my family who disappeared."

The comet streaked behind a dark cloud. The sky looked golden. The wind blew harder and the ship rocked violently.

"It's funny, the things that go through your mind," Jim said. "I remember a preacher at our church talking about the *Titanic*. He said there were only two types of people on that boat: those who were saved and those who were lost at sea."

John nodded.

"The guy asked what we'd do if we only had an hour to live. I went out in the parking lot with my friends. We made fun of him. Now I wish I'd have listened."

The comet appeared again, a huge, burning ball of smoke and flame. Men on deck shuddered and cried out.

"Let's go down there," John said. He looked at the captain and nodded, but the man didn't return his gaze.

John led the way to the deck, shielding his face and trying to keep his balance. Others who had the mark followed. At the center of the ship, the men joined hands and knelt. The crashing of waves didn't drown out John's voice.

"God, I thank you that you're true to your word, that what you say happens. I pray right now you would give us the strength to go through this and that you would bring others to yourself."

Men prayed. Some yelled, "Help us!"

As the comet neared the surface of the water, the sky peeled back, revealing a smoking trail miles long. The heat from the object singed hair and melted John's watchband. He peeled it off and threw it over the edge.

The wind died. The comet reached the horizon and fell out of sight. Then the most

terrifying sound. An explosion on the surface
of the water.

Vicki covered her mouth with a hand as the
GC plane transmitted images of the impact.
The water boiled from the intense heat and
steam rose, along with water spouts and
typhoons. The plane broadcasting the event
was knocked out of the sky by the force of
the impact.

"They're gonna be showing this video for
a long time," Lionel said.

John grabbed a metal post and hung on. The
sky surged in turmoil. The captain shouted
over the loudspeaker for the men to remain
calm. Some grabbed extra life preservers and
jumped overboard.

John calculated that the ship's position
was two hundred miles east of the comet.
A few minutes after he lost sight of the
comet, the ship was drawn backward toward
the splashdown site. Water surged around
them. It felt like he was a kid standing at the
edge of the beach, the tide rushing around
his feet.

Part of him wanted to go below deck and hide, but John couldn't stop watching God's mighty judgment. The ship gathered speed and surged along, powered only by the turbulent ocean. Men were swept overboard as they stood and felt the awesome wind. There was no sound but the howling of the wind and the thundering of water.

Then John saw it. It started on the horizon and slowly rose as the ship rushed toward it. A wave so huge it seemed to scrape the clouds. Blue water rose skyward. John had seen pictures of waves that looked like canyons, with boats nothing but specks. But he had never seen anything like this. The blue turned to red. The bloody water churned all around the ship. It splashed on board. John felt it ooze down his back. He rubbed the liquid between his fingers. It was thick and sticky.

The thought of drowning had terrified John as a child. Now, he felt a sense of peace. *I'm ready for home, God,* he prayed.

The ship sped on, men screaming when they caught sight of the wave. John looked at Jim and nodded. Nothing to say and no one to hear it if you did.

The wave blotted out the sky. The ship rose against it, then turned slightly and rolled. John held on to the metal pipe as the ship plunged into the water. Submerged, the blood stung his eyes. He was in what felt like an underwater typhoon. Bodies and ship and equipment became one with the wave.

In the sea of red, John held his breath. The pressure of the water was unbearable. Seconds later he tried to breathe.

No air. John reached for the surface, but he felt miles away. Panic. Blackness.

Then light. Blessed light.

Judd gasped as newscasters described the devastation. Hovering aircraft showed America's Atlantic coast. Billions of tons of water crashed onto homes and businesses up to fifty miles inland. The remains of shrimp boats were scattered over roadways. An oil freighter, whose crew had been plucked from the deck by a helicopter just in time, lay on a mountainside in Virginia. A plane flew over the area where the old man had refused to leave his house. It was completely underwater.

Judd tried to think of something to say to Mark, but couldn't. Vicki shouted for Mark to come to the computer. "It's from John!"

Judd read over Mark's shoulder.

Incredible opportunity to give the message,

John had written. *Nothing like a killer comet to wake you to reality.*

Some day I hope you meet Carl. He can tell you what happened here. No time now. Just enough to say I love you all. Keep fighting the good fight. We'll be cheering you on. Never give up. John.

Judd put his face in his hands.

"He probably died within minutes after sending that," Mark said.

Vicki and Shelly held each other and cried. Lionel put a hand on Mark's shoulder.

"You had a great cousin," Lionel said.

Mark nodded. "I know."

Nicolae Carpathia responded to the crisis with a grim face. In another address to the world he revealed that all travel would be affected by the damage. The meeting of the Jewish witnesses would be postponed another ten weeks.

"The loss of any human life is tragic," Carpathia said. "We grieve with the families whose loved ones perished in this latest catastrophe. However, our experts were correct. Had we attempted to explode the object, many more lives would have been lost.

"But we can do something in memory of

those who died. We can rebuild. Travel routes and cities that have been wiped out will be restored. Let this hardship draw us together to create a new world that loves peace."

In response to the potentate, the two witnesses at the Wailing Wall went on the offensive. Judd and the others watched on the Internet as Moishe and Eli boiled in anger.

"Behold, the land of Israel will continue to be dry, as it has been since the signing of the unholy treaty!" Moishe said.

Eli picked up the message. "Any threat to the evangelists who are sealed will be met with rivers of blood!" he said.

To prove their power was from the Almighty, Moishe and Eli called upon God to let it rain only on the Temple Mount for seven minutes. From a clear, blue sky came a sheet of rain. The dust turned to mud. Televised reports showed families running from their homes, laughing and dancing. They believed their crops were saved. But seven minutes later the rain stopped. The mud returned to dust. The people were speechless.

"Woe unto you, mockers of the one true God!" Eli and Moishe shouted. "Until the due time, when God allows us to be felled and later returns us to his side, you shall have no power over us or over those God has called to proclaim his name throughout the earth!"

FIVE

Mr. Stein's Questions

THE comet affected weather around the globe. Vicki watched thick clouds roll into the Midwest. The news reported a tornado warning.

Vicki knew Mark was grieving John, but she didn't know what to do when he went off by himself. She offered to get him food, but he waved her away.

Judd and Mr. Stein were at the computer.

"People are begging to know God," Judd said. "I don't think Tsion has time to—"

"If he does not have time, he does not have to talk," Mr. Stein said.

"He's already talked to you," Judd said.

"Judd, if I am one of the 144,000 evangelists described in the Bible, I want to know," Mr. Stein said. "And I think Rabbi Ben-Judah will welcome a conversation."

Judd logged on and tried to contact Tsion. Vicki saw hundreds of messages. "Are those all questions for the rabbi?" Vicki said.

"They're waiting to be answered," Judd said. "I did as many as I could last night—"

A beep interrupted Judd. Vicki was excited to see the face of Tsion Ben-Judah on the screen. Judd gave Tsion an update about the kids. Tsion was saddened to hear about John. "He is another of the tribulation martyrs," Tsion said.

Judd introduced Mr. Stein, who leaned toward the camera and waved. Mr. Stein was shaking with excitement.

"I am glad to see you," Tsion said.

"My brother," Mr. Stein said, "I had to get in touch once more. I want to know if I am a Witness and what my assignment will be."

"I'm afraid only God can reveal that," the rabbi said. "I urge you to come to the meeting."

"Perhaps I could go with you," Mr. Stein said.

Judd flinched.

"I'm afraid that would be impossible," Tsion said. "Thousands of people are pleading with me to come to their countries and train them face-to-face. The Meeting of the Witnesses is designed to accomplish this.

"God is working out the details. The first

twenty-five thousand to arrive will gather in Teddy Kollek Stadium. The rest will watch on closed-circuit television at sites all over the Holy Land. I will invite Moishe and Eli to join us. It will be a great time of teaching and learning."

Mr. Stein looked dejected. "I had hoped you could help me personally," he said.

"You have me now," Tsion said. "What are you concerned about?"

Mr. Stein glanced at Vicki and Judd. "I have doubts," he said. "I believe that Jesus is God, that he died for me. But I feel so unworthy. At times I think I will somehow go back to my old life. I fear God could not possibly use me."

"You struggle with sin," Tsion said. "You think you should be perfect and you are not."

"Exactly."

Tsion smiled. "The apostle Paul struggled with the same thing. Read Romans, chapter 7. You are not perfect and never will be until you are with God."

"But at times I do not even feel like I am a follower of Christ."

"Your enemy is at work. He does not want you to follow Christ. This struggle shows you are not falling away. Just the opposite. As you grow in your faith, you will see more of your sin. How much you care about yourself. It is happening to me every day.

"But this fight is not a sign of defeat. God is working in you."

Mr. Stein nodded. "But what if I don't feel like—?"

"Feelings are always difficult," Tsion said. "Do not base your faith on your feelings. Instead, read what God says in his Word about you. If you have asked God to forgive you and come into your life, he has.

"Second Corinthians 5:17 says you are a new person. God has begun a new life in you. Romans 15:7 says you have been accepted by Christ. When God looks at you, he no longer sees your sin. He sees the perfection of Jesus.

"In Romans, chapter 8, Paul asks, 'Can anything ever separate us from Christ's love?'" Tsion paused. "Do you have trouble? Are you in danger from the Global Community? Paul says, 'Despite all these things, overwhelming victory is ours through Christ, who loved us.'"

Mr. Stein rubbed his forehead. "But how could God love that way? I have done terrible things."

Tsion smiled. "We judge people by *our* standard. When you believe in your heart that Jesus died for you and was raised from the dead, God views you no longer as an enemy, but as a son.

"The Scriptures are clear. God is working in you to do the good things he planned for you. You are kept not by your own power to do good things, but by his love and mercy."

Mr. Stein nodded. "I have many more questions."

"I'm sure," Tsion said. "Continue studying. See if what I say is true. It is clear now. The world is taking sides. Many people will follow the Antichrist. But many will believe in God's only Son. It is our job to take that message to everyone."

Vicki felt encouraged by Tsion's talk with Mr. Stein. Before he signed off she asked about Chloe.

"She is making great improvement," Tsion said. "Wait right there."

Vicki watched Chloe hobble to Tsion's computer. She smiled when she saw Vicki. "I want you to know how saddened I was about Ryan," Chloe said.

"What happened to you?" Vicki said.

"Long story," Chloe said. "When the earthquake hit, I ran from Loretta's house. Someone found me and transported me to a Wisconsin hospital. Buck caught up to me in

Minneapolis. The GC had some kind of plan, but we were able to escape."

"Is it true about you having a baby?" Vicki said.

Chloe beamed. "It's true," she said. "Buck's acting like a mother hen, but we're both really excited."

Vicki asked about Chloe's father, Captain Rayford Steele.

"Pray for him," Chloe said. "Amanda's body was found in the plane wreckage. He had to dive into the Tigris River. Her death really shook him up."

Chloe said hello to Judd and the others. Judd asked about Buck and what happened in Denver. "Is he really being charged with murder?"

Chloe whispered something to Tsion. The rabbi nodded. Chloe said, "Buck went there to get Hattie Durham. She's pregnant with Nicolae Carpathia's child."

Vicki gasped.

"The Global Community is after Hattie," Chloe said. "Buck went to rescue her. He hit a guard in self-defense after the guard killed a staff worker. The guard died. They blame Buck, but it's not true."

"Is Hattie okay?" Vicki said.

"As well as can be expected," Chloe said. "We've got a new member of the Trib Force.

A doctor. He's been helping both of us as we try to recover."

"Is Buck still working for Carpathia?" Judd said.

"He's putting the magazine together on the Internet," Chloe said. "He doesn't know how much longer he can work for such an evil man."

Vicki wanted to talk with Chloe about Judd. Vicki had remained cordial to him, but she felt something brewing under the surface. Chloe asked about the kids' escape from the GC and heard the story of Mr. Stein.

"We really need your help with E-mail," Chloe said. "Some of the messages are people saying they're praying. But many need replies."

"As soon as we figure out our next move," Judd said, "we'll get two or three people on it."

Chloe thanked them. "I miss having you guys around. I wish we could keep you here."

"We understand," Vicki said. "I hope we can talk more sometime."

Chloe gave them her cell phone number for an emergency. Tsion prayed for the kids and closed the connection.

Vicki heard a rumble of engines. Pete, who had been sleeping in the back of the service station, ran to the front. He cursed, then looked at the kids. "Sorry. You guys are going to have to hide again."

"What's going—," Judd said.

"No time to explain," Pete interrupted. "Hide."

Judd and the others climbed into the oil-changing bay while Boyd parked a car overhead. The room was dark and smelled like gasoline.

"I wish we could see what's happening," Lionel said. "You think it's Red back with the GC?"

"Pete said Red wouldn't bother us," Judd said. "I don't know who it could be."

Judd whispered to Boyd, but the man said, "Keep quiet. There's a GC guy out front."

A few minutes later someone came inside. Judd heard angry voices. Finally, motorcycles started and drove away. Boyd moved the car, and the kids climbed out.

"What?" Judd said.

The manager bit his lip. "I don't know what to tell you," he said. "Pete said he had to go with the GC."

"I heard what happened," another biker said. It was Sally, who had given Vicki a ride to escape the commander. "I talked with Pete this morning. Had to drag it out of him, but he finally told me.

"Red was going to report you guys. Pete wanted to catch up to him and talk him out of it. When he did, Red freaked. He drove wild and tried to force Pete off the road. Pete yelled at him, but Red wouldn't stop.

"Red and Clyde, the guy with the gold teeth, both forced Pete onto a road that leads to a rock quarry," Sally continued. "Red tried to cut Pete off, but Red lost control of his bike. He hit Clyde, and they both went over the edge. I guess it was hundreds of feet to the bottom and nothing but rock."

"How awful," Vicki said.

"But the GC think Pete killed them?" Judd said.

Sally shrugged. "Pete said he'd show the GC where Red and Clyde fell. I hope they believe his story."

Judd frowned. If the GC suspected Pete, they would return.

"Everybody get ready to move," Judd said. He dialed the number Boyd had given him.

"This is Zeke," an older man said.

"I'm looking for your son," Judd said.

"What for?"

"We were told he could help us," Judd said. "We're in some trouble."

The man yelled, "Z!" and a moment later Zeke Jr. was on the phone. He seemed cautious and asked who had recommended him. Judd told him and Zeke Jr. laughed. "Boyd? That old coot?"

"Can you help us?" Judd said.

"I don't know you from Adam," Zeke Jr. said.

"The Global Community is on our tail," Judd said. "It's only a matter of time until they find us."

Zeke Jr. paused. "I think I can scrounge up some papers for you," he said. "As far as changing your faces, we'll have to see. When?"

"Tonight," Judd said.

"Whoa," Zeke Jr. said. "That's a little fast. There's bad weather between you and me. Tornadoes."

"Any way you can come to us?" Judd said.

"Not a chance," Zeke Jr. said. "You come to me or I pass."

Judd gave him the name and descriptions of each of the members. "When will you be ready for us?" he said.

"Make it before sunup," he said.

SIX

Zeke's Place

JUDD gathered what the kids would need for their trip. He asked Taylor Graham to help Mr. Stein locate his hidden money, but Taylor refused.

"I'll go," Mark said.

"If Pete doesn't come back, I'm going for him," Taylor said.

Conrad frowned. "You're gonna get the Global Community any way you can."

"That's right."

"You're gonna get yourself killed," Conrad said. "Pete can take care of himself."

Taylor smirked. "You don't get it. I'm not just going to get the GC back for what they've done; I'm gonna stop them."

"If you really want to do damage," Conrad said sarcastically, "why don't you kill Nicolae Carpathia?" Taylor stared at Conrad. "You wouldn't try anything that stupid, would you?"

Judd couldn't believe what he was hearing. "You don't need revenge."

Taylor rolled his eyes. "I know, I need God. Well he's never done anything for me. If you guys want to play your Bible games and try to figure out what's happening next, fine."

Darrion Stahley stepped forward. "I've known you since I was a kid. You're smart. Hasn't any of this sunk in? The disappearances? The earthquake?"

"I know your mom and dad are dead, little lady," Taylor said. "And the Global Community's responsible. I'll stop them if it's the last thing I do."

"God saved your neck for a reason," Conrad said. "Don't waste an opportunity—"

"I saved my own neck," Taylor snapped. "I don't believe you people. If you want to get something done, you do it yourself. You don't wait for some god to do it for you."

"That's enough," Judd said, looking at Conrad and Darrion. "He's free to make his choice." Judd turned to Taylor. "We could use a pilot."

Taylor looked away. "If I can help you, I will. But I don't promise anything."

"Fair enough," Judd said.

The wind howled. Tree branches scraped the windows of the gas station. "We leave at midnight," Judd said. "Hopefully we'll be at Zeke's place by sunup."

Vicki heard voices. Crying. Kids ran through the woods in front of her. Someone waved her forward. A boy. She could only see the back of his head. It looked like Ryan.

Breathing hard, Vicki tried to catch up. The woods were dense. She could see her breath in the crisp air. She wanted to turn back, find safety, but she couldn't let the kids down. She kept going.

Someone was after the kids, after her. She turned around but no one was there.

Clouds hid the stars. Hard to see. One foot in front of the other. A branch. A fallen tree. She fell and scraped a knee.

Then flickering light in the distance. She stood and limped toward it.

She reached the clearing and saw a few kids bounding across a meadow toward a building. Others gathered on a second-floor balcony.

Vicki heard movement to her left and saw the boy running toward her. Behind him were soldiers. Vicki screamed.

Vicki followed the boy, scared. Kids lined the

balcony, waving to her. "Run," they shouted. "Come on!"

The light was coming from the house. Beams shone through windows. "I don't understand!" she shouted at the boy.

"What's to understand?" he said.

It sounded like Ryan. She ran faster.

"What is that place?" Vicki said.

The boy didn't answer but kept running. Vicki glanced behind her. When she turned, the boy was gone.

"Hurry!" someone said from above.

Vicki reached the steps. The soldiers stopped, turned around, and went back into the woods.

"Why did they leave?" Vicki said.

"Why did who leave?" Shelly said, shaking Vicki awake. "Come on, time to go."

Vicki rubbed her eyes and followed Shelly outside. Members of Pete's group had loaned their bikes. Darrion rode with Judd. *Good,* Vicki thought. She put on a helmet and sat behind Conrad. Lionel rode alone on the third bike.

"Good luck," Shelly said. "I hope I don't recognize you when you get back."

Conrad followed Judd. Vicki relaxed and thought about the boy in her dream. Did she miss Ryan that badly? Could it be some kind of message?

"Did Mark and Mr. Stein leave?" Vicki yelled to Conrad.

"Half hour ago," Conrad said. "Pete's still not back."

The wind had blown down makeshift power lines. Judd held up a hand, and the kids carefully drove around the dangerous wires.

"What happens if we run into GC?" Vicki said.

"Judd said we'll try to outrun them," Conrad said. "I hope we don't have to."

The kids stayed away from main roads, even going across fields. By early morning Vicki was tired of all the ruts and ridges. She was glad to find paved roads again, even though they still had huge cracks from the earthquake. Dogs barked as they rode through neighborhoods.

Vicki told Conrad her dream. "What do you think it means?" she said.

"Could mean you haven't been getting enough sleep," Conrad said. "Then again, it might be God trying to tell you something."

"What?" Vicki said.

Conrad shrugged.

Judd stopped and turned off his motor. They were on the edge of what had once been downtown Des Plaines. The streets were deserted. A light was on in a broken-down one-pump gas station.

"Let me check it out," Conrad said. "I'll signal if it's okay."

Judd nodded. Conrad crept toward the filling station. A few minutes later Vicki saw a light flash inside.

Zeke Jr. opened the creaky garage door and the kids pushed their cycles inside. Zeke Jr. was in his mid-twenties, had long hair, and was covered with tattoos. He wore black cowboy boots, black jeans, and a black leather vest over bare arms and flabby chest.

"People call me Z," Zeke Jr. said as he looked at each of their foreheads. "I guess 'cause it's easier."

Judd said, "Where's all your equipment for—"

"I know it dudn't look like much," Z said. "By the time I'm through, this place'll be a shopping center for believers."

Vicki looked around the station. Dirty rags lay on black oil drums. There were out-of-date calendars with pictures of cars. An oily phone book lay on a counter. Everything looked grimy. Vicki wondered how they could trust someone who kept such a dingy business.

Z seemed to read her mind. He grinned. "Follow me," he said. Z led them to a tiny washroom. The sign said Danger. High Voltage. Do Not Touch.

"Anybody puts a hand on here and they get a little buzz," Z said. "Not enough to hurt, just make 'em think twice. Come on."

Z knew where to push. The panel opened and Z slid it out of the way. He led the five kids down a wooden staircase to his shelter. It was fashioned out of the earth beneath and behind the station. Deep in the back Vicki saw boxes of food, medicine, bottled water, and assorted supplies.

"If you guys need anything back there, let me know," Z said.

The room had no windows and was cool. *Perfect*, Vicki thought, *to keep the food and medicine fresh.* A TV news broadcast was on low in the background. Beside the TV was a dog-eared spiral notebook and a laptop.

"When I'm done, we'll need to get a picture," Z said. As he set up his camera he told the kids his story.

"Before all this I did a few tattoos, pinstriped cars and trucks, airbrushed some T-shirts, and even painted murals on some 18-wheelers. That business dried up a long time ago."

"What happened to the rest of your family?" Vicki said.

"My dad, Zeke, runs the station," Z said, fiddling with the camera. "My mom and two sisters died in a fire the night of the disappearances. We were tryin' to get over that when this friend of my dad's, a long-haul trucker, comes through. Starts talkin' 'bout God and his plan. I didn't buy it at first. The more he talked, the more it made sense. He gave us a Bible, and we started reading in Revelation, of all places.

"I don't mind tellin' ya, I've done a lot of drugs. When I wasn't smokin' or shootin' up, I was drinkin'. I'd stay high until I needed some more money; then I'd go back to work a few days.

"God got hold of both of us. My dad and I go to an underground church in Arlington Heights now. I want to be a major supplier to Christians. Hopefully, with my contacts with truckers, we'll turn this place into a warehouse for believers."

"You mean you'll ship stuff from here?" Judd said.

"With what's ahead, somebody's gotta do it," Z said. He pointed to the computer. "Rabbi says it's gonna get worse and worse. We have to prepare."

Z tacked a sheet on the wall. "Before I take your pictures," he said, "we gotta figure out

what to do with you." He looked at Vicki.
"That's not your natural color, is it?"

Vicki shook her head. "Red."

"The hair's okay, then," Z said. He put on
plastic gloves and opened a desk drawer.
Inside were dental materials. He fitted a
device over Vicki's front teeth. They stuck out
a little and seemed to change the shape of
her face.

"You should be able to leave this on all the
time, once you get used to it," Z said.

"Incredible," Lionel said. "What can you
do for me?"

"You're a challenge," Z said. "We'll shave
your head to start. Then a scar on your face
might draw some attention. Sunglasses,
maybe."

Z worked on the kids' appearances. He
changed hair color, cut hair, and added scars
and tattoos that amazed the kids. When he
was finished he took their pictures.

A bell rang above. "Dad's probably still
asleep," Z said. "Let me get that and I'll be
right back."

Z unlocked the station and helped a
customer with fuel. When he returned he
squatted behind an old couch and swung
open a rickety filing cabinet. He grabbed a
cardboard box filled with different types of

identification. Some were driver's licenses.
Some were student IDs.

"Sorry I'm not too organized yet," Z said.

"Where did you get those?" Vicki said.

Z slammed the filing cabinet shut with his
boot. "The earthquake claimed a lotta lives.
These weren't doing the dead any good, and
they could sure help out our cause in the
future."

Vicki looked at the faces and names scattered throughout the box. "All of these
people are dead?" she said.

Z nodded. "I get the wallets before the GC
gets the body." He dumped the contents
onto a table. "Don't go by the faces," he said.
"Try to find somebody who's close to your
age."

Vicki rummaged through the cards and
found a girl a year older than she and about
the same height.

"Jackie Browne," Z said. "Looks good.
She's an organ donor, too. Good citizen of
the Global Community."

"How much can we change on this?" Judd
said.

"If you want me to get this done today,
you have to take it the way you find it," Z
said. "Give me a couple of days and I can
make you a member of Enigma Babylon, or
even a GC soldier."

"We don't have that kind of time," Judd said.

Lionel found a smaller box on the filing cabinet. "What's this?" he said.

"Those are from this week," Z said. "I don't use ones that fresh."

Lionel rummaged through the box and gave a low whistle. "Look at this."

The kids crowded around. The military ID card showed a stocky man with medals and decorations. Beside his picture it read *Commander Terrell Blancka.*

"I remember that one," Z said. "Strange. Found him in a culvert near a church, or what was left of it. Looked like an execution. Gunshot wound."

"I thought he was being reassigned," Vicki said.

"He was," Lionel said. "Permanently."

Vicki glanced at the stack of cards and gasped. Among them was Joyce's, the girl who had accused Vicki of murdering Mrs. Jenness. "Do you know how she died?" Vicki said.

Z shook his head. "I've got a friend at one of the GC morgues," he said. "A believer. I got that one from him."

Vicki felt a sudden sense of relief. If her accuser was dead, she was off the hook for the murder rap. Then Vicki felt a wave of guilt. Joyce had heard about God but rejected him.

Z gave the kids blankets and showed them an area where they could rest. Vicki was exhausted. She watched Z through the doorway as he turned on his magnifying light and began cutting the pictures. From this day on she would be Jackie Browne.

SEVEN

Vicki's Discovery

MARK thought about John as he drove beside Mr. Stein. The video of the comet's crash kept flashing in Mark's mind. It was so spectacular that the networks would run the footage for weeks. Reports of lost boats had filled the news. Mark had logged on to the list of crew members on the *Peacekeeper 1* and found John's name.

He was so engrossed in his thoughts that he didn't realize he had lost Mr. Stein. Mark turned the motorcycle around and back-tracked. He found the man and his cycle in a ditch.

"I must have hit the accelerator instead of the brake," Mr. Stein said, limping away from the bike.

"Climb on," Mark said.

Mr. Stein hobbled onto the back of Mark's motorcycle.

"Is the money in cash?" Mark said.

"Large bills," Mr. Stein said. "I hope we can take it in one load. . . . Are you thinking about your cousin?"

Mark nodded.

"I am sorry for your pain," Mr. Stein said. "I was just reading the passage where Jesus said those who mourn are blessed."

"If that's so, you've had a double helping," Mark said.

"Tsion teaches about this," Mr. Stein said. "He points those who are struggling with the death of loved ones to the end of Revelation. God says he will remove all sorrows, and there will be no more death or crying or pain."

"Can't wait for that," Mark said. "But I gotta be honest. I don't understand why God would let all this happen."

"You have been a believer longer than I have," Mr. Stein said. "I should be asking you these questions."

The two rode in silence. Mr. Stein pointed the way. When they got close he said, "My office is on the next street. Stop here."

Mark pulled to the curb. Businesses were in shambles. A construction crew had cleared the road of debris, but the sidewalk was twisted.

"The GC might still be guarding your place," Mark said.

Mr. Stein nodded and gestured for Mark to follow him. They squeezed between two buildings and checked for cars near Mr. Stein's office.

"I don't see why we're risking this," Mark said. "If your money's hidden somewhere else, let's go there."

Mr. Stein pointed to a broken window in the bottom floor of his office. "We'll crawl through there," he said.

"But—"

"My money is here," Mr. Stein said, "if the Global Community didn't take it."

Mark followed Mr. Stein and kept watch. They passed a wall safe, its door lying broken on the floor.

"Just as I suspected," Mr. Stein said.

They moved upstairs. Mr. Stein pointed to desks with missing computers. "Either vandals or the GC," he said.

They reached a second-floor office with a couch and desk. The computer tower was gone, but the old monitor was still on the desk.

"Good," Mr. Stein said.

Mark watched in amazement as Mr. Stein unscrewed the back of the monitor.

"I was on the phone with Judd when he alerted me there was a bug," Mr. Stein said. "I had already hidden the money, but I wanted whoever was listening to think otherwise."

Mr. Stein took out the last screw and opened the back of the monitor. The contents of the monitor had been removed, and the space was crammed with bills. The man pulled out wads of hundreds. Mark had never seen so much money in his life.

Glass broke downstairs. Someone cursed. Two voices. One of them said, "Got almost everything last night. There's still some computer stuff upstairs."

Mr. Stein looked wildly at Mark.

Footsteps banged on the stairs.

"Quick, help me put the money in the drawer," Mr. Stein whispered.

They dumped the cash in the drawer and fumbled with the back of the computer. At the top of the stairs the footsteps stopped. Another man, this one with a squeaky voice, said, "I thought you said this place was deserted."

"Come on," the other said.

Mr. Stein motioned for Mark to get behind the door. When the two came into view, Mark was safely out of sight. Mr. Stein sat in a chair, his feet on the desk.

"Welcome, gentlemen," Mr. Stein said cheerily. "I'm glad to see you're back."

Squeaky Voice was short and walked with a slight limp. The other man was tall and thin. He looked like the picture of Ichabod Crane Mark had seen in his reading book as a kid.

"Who are you?" Squeaky said.

"I'm the proprietor of this establishment," Mr. Stein said. The two stared at him. "The owner," Mr. Stein explained. "This is my office."

Mark noticed Ichabod had a gun. Mr. Stein pointed to it and said, "There's no need for violence. You're welcome to whatever you'd like."

Squeaky squinted and jerked his head sideways. "You *want* us to take stuff?"

Mr. Stein smiled. "When I found the office standing, with all the other buildings on this block in ruins, I was shocked. The insurance won't pay unless there was real damage. But now that you boys have 'cleaned up' for me, I should be paid quite a bit."

Squeaky still didn't understand.

"He's in it for the insurance money," Ichabod explained.

"Did you find the safe downstairs?" Mr. Stein said.

"Oh yeah, that was a piece o' cake," Squeaky said.

"How about the telephone equipment in the basement?" Mr. Stein said.

"Didn't know there was a basement," Ichabod said.

Mr. Stein pointed them toward the correct door, and the thieves left. Mr. Stein followed them. Mark opened the drawer and stuffed the money into a black satchel. When Mr. Stein returned he said, "We must hurry. There is no telephone equipment down there."

Mark cleaned out the drawer. The satchel was full and very heavy. Mr. Stein grabbed the satchel and raced down the stairs, Mark right behind him. Mark was almost out the window when he heard Ichabod shout, "Hey, there's two of them!"

The sun was coming up as Mark raced toward the alley. A shot rang out. A bullet pinged against a brick wall nearby. Mark took the satchel from Mr. Stein, who was lagging behind, and ran for the bike. By the time Mr. Stein made it, Mark had the motorcycle roaring. Mr. Stein clutched the satchel tightly to his chest as Mark sped away.

Vicki awoke first and, peeking through the doorway, found Z still at work on the IDs.

Judd was now Leland Brayfield. Conrad found the driver's license of James Lindley, two years older. Darrion had become Rosemary Bishop. But it was more difficult for Lionel. Z admitted his stash of African-American IDs was lacking. The closest Lionel could come was a twenty-five-year-old who was at least fifty pounds heavier. Z said making too many changes to "Greg Butler" could tip off whoever scanned Lionel's new ID, but he would do it anyway.

Z was laminating Lionel's card when Vicki shuffled into the room. She yawned and sat by his desk. It was nearly noon.

"You've been at it quite a while," Vicki said.

"Not so bad," Z said, pulling the magnifying light down to inspect the card. He handed "Jackie Browne's" card to her.

Vicki gasped. "This is amazing," she said.

Z blushed. "Where are you guys headed from here?"

Vicki laughed. "Who knows? We've been fighting about our next move since we escaped the GC."

"What kinda choices you got?"

"Darrion's folks have a place in Wisconsin," Vicki said. "It'd be good for us to get away from Chicago, but . . ."

Z nodded and opened a packet of beef jerky. He leaned back in his chair as he chewed. Rolls of fat jiggled under his black vest. "Who says you guys have to stay together?"

Vicki paused. The Young Trib Force had been separated before, but it had never been their choice.

"If you guys are fighting about what to do," Z said, "split up. You may be able to do more good apart."

"What do you mean?" Vicki said.

"I'm helping people get supplies and fuel," Z said, "and keepin' the Global Community out of your hair. If the rabbi's right, pretty soon more and more people are going to need supplies, which means more people will have to help. I could use somebody right here in the office."

Vicki admired Z and his dad, but she couldn't imagine working for them. But something stirred in her as he spoke.

Z picked up a notebook by his laptop and turned to the back. Vicki couldn't read a word of the scratching. "I'll tell you another thing that's gonna happen," he said. "With parents raptured or dead, a lot more young people like you are gonna be on the run. Especially believers."

Vicki looked straight at Z and said, "The dream."

"What's that?" Z said.

"I had this dream," Vicki said. "I was running through woods, following a boy. The GC was chasing us. We ran down by a river and came into a clearing and saw a huge house. There were kids on the balcony, waving and calling. When I made it to the front door, the GC stopped. It was like I disappeared. Then—"

"This is spooky," Z said, sitting forward, the chair legs slamming on the floor. He opened a desk drawer and rummaged through some papers.

"Tell me what the house looked like," Z said.

"I don't remember except that it had a balcony and was really long," Vicki said. "I think there was some kind of pole in front. Like a flagpole."

Z stared at her. "I don't believe it."

He rummaged through another drawer and moved to the filing cabinet.

"What is it?" Vicki said.

Z snapped a piece of paper from a file. "Got it!" he said.

He handed Vicki a ten-year-old real estate listing. Statistics covered the bottom half of the page. Fifty acres, zoned residential, well water, etc. On the top half was a picture that took Vicki's breath away. The photo was fuzzy, but it looked exactly like the house Vicki had seen in her dream, even though the house was blocked by trees.

"It even has the flagpole," Z said, pointing to the right side of the picture.

"What is it?" Vicki said when she caught her breath.

"An old boarding school," Z said. "About forty miles south of here. My grandpa bought it from the state. Hadn't been used in years. He didn't do much with it. Then he died and left it my dad. Nearly sold it a few times, but the buyers always backed out."

Z pointed to a brown streak behind the house. "And it's in a flood plain," he said. "Right next to a river."

"What are you going to do with it?" Vicki said.

"It's not that far from a major trucking route. Plan is to store supplies there. We already have some meds, food, water—that kind of thing."

"Won't it attract attention?" Vicki said.

Z pulled out another sheet of paper. Along the top was written *Condemned*.

"This document says the place is a hazard and people should stay away. Some of the neighbors think the place is haunted. They don't come around."

Vicki scratched her head. "You're going to think this is stupid," she said.

"Go ahead; I'm listening."

"For a long time I've had this idea of a place where kids can go," Vicki said. She stood. Thoughts swirled in her mind. Ideas came fast. "What if we use this as a training center for the Young Trib Force? What if kids who want to know the truth come there to study? We could make it a distribution center for all your food and medicine, too."

Vicki could see it, a fulfillment of her dream. Z put his hands behind his head and listened.

"It's far enough away that the Global Community wouldn't find us," Vicki continued, "but close enough to help believers who need supplies."

"What would that mean for the rest of the group?" Z said. "If some want to go to Wisconsin or they don't like the school idea, what happens then?"

Vicki turned and saw Judd in the doorway. He looked funny with all his changes. But Vicki didn't smile.

"I guess we'll each have to make our own decision," Vicki said.

EIGHT

The Search for Phoenix

JUDD didn't like Vicki's idea. Something about taking over the school bothered him. The others awoke and joined them.

"You're taking for granted that Z is offering," Judd said.

Z handed him some beef jerky. Judd declined.

"This place has been in the family for years," Z said. "I'd have to ask my dad, but I see it as a win-win. You guys get a place to stay, and we get someone to watch the supplies."

"What about Wisconsin?" Darrion said.

"Everybody has to choose," Vicki said. "We can't force people to join us."

"You're talking about splitting up the group," Judd said.

"You don't like it because it wasn't your idea," Vicki said.

"That's not true!" Judd shouted.

Lionel held up a hand. "Hold it! What's important isn't whose idea it is; it's that we respect each other."

Vicki explained the school option to the whole group. Darrion held up a hand. "Wisconsin reminds me of my parents, but Vicki's idea sounds good. If God gave her that dream, maybe we should do it."

Judd looked at Vicki. "I'm not trying to shoot this down. I don't think we can base an important decision like this on a dream."

Vicki squinted. "Remember when you went to Israel to check on Nina and Dan? Wasn't that partly because you'd had a dream about them?"

"That was different," Judd said.

"Forget the dream," Lionel said. "We need a place that's safe, and it sounds like we can help Z and his dad with supplies."

Z nodded. "I can't say when we'll start running. Let me go talk with my dad." Z left.

Lionel looked at Conrad. "What do you think about all this?"

Conrad pursed his lips. "I don't know. I'm mixed up. Makes you wonder if God's really helping us, or if we're trying to do this on our own."

"What do you mean?" Vicki said.

Conrad swatted at a fly. "If we're all on the same team, why do we argue so much?"

"Just because we disagree doesn't mean we're not on the same team," Lionel said.

Vicki scooted closer to Conrad. "Is it deeper than that?"

"What Mr. Stein said to Tsion," Conrad said. "I just don't know if this is real."

"You heard what Tsion said to Mr. Stein, right?" Judd said.

"What if I turn away?" Conrad said. "What if I go with Taylor and try to kill Nicolae, or just turn my back on the whole thing?"

Z came back in the room. "Good news—"

Judd held up a hand and pulled out his pocket Bible. "Let's go over this again. John, chapter 1. Everyone who believes in Jesus and accepts him becomes a child of God. They are reborn."

Conrad nodded.

"John, chapter 3 says everyone who believes in Jesus has eternal life, and chapter 5 says those who believe will never be condemned for their sins, but they have already passed from death to life.

"Romans 10 says if you confess with your mouth that Jesus is Lord and believe in your heart that God raised him from the dead, you will be saved."

Conrad read the verses with Judd.

Vicki spoke up. "I've been reading Revelation to see what's ahead. I love the verses that talk about the Book of Life. When you believed, Conrad, your name was written there. God knows you."

"So I can't un-save myself?" Conrad said.

Judd smiled. "When you asked God into your life, he saved you by his power. And he'll keep you by his power. It doesn't mean you won't have doubts or you won't sin." Judd looked at Vicki. "And it doesn't mean you'll always treat your brothers and sisters the way you should."

Conrad was silent. Finally, Z said, "My dad thinks your idea about the school's great."

Vicki took the key and the directions to the old schoolhouse. "One more thing," she said. "I want to look for Phoenix."

Judd shut his eyes and held his tongue.

"You mean the dog that was with you?" Conrad said. "I might know where he is."

"Can I talk with you for a minute?" Judd said to Vicki. "Alone?"

Vicki climbed up the narrow staircase and entered the gas station in front of Judd. Z's father was with a customer.

"If you kids only wanted to use the rest room, you have to buy something," Zeke said.

"Yes, sir," Judd said. He picked up a couple of candy bars from a cardboard bin on the counter and left two bills by the cash register.

"Teenagers," the customer said in disgust.

Vicki knew Zeke was covering for them. The customer didn't have the mark of the believer. This is what it would be like. To stay alive, they would have to be careful with everyone without the mark.

Judd handed Vicki the candy bar and they walked outside. Vicki blew dust from the wrapper. Clouds blocked the sun and a hazy gloom hung over the area.

"I didn't want to talk about it in front of the others," Judd said.

"You don't want me going for Phoenix," Vicki said.

"What I want or don't want isn't the point. You saw what Conrad's going through."

"Which is exactly why this school would be such a good idea," Vicki said. "Kids need to understand what the Bible really teaches."

"There's nothing wrong with the idea, but why can't kids get the same thing from Tsion's Web site?"

"They can get information there, but I

think they need a person to show them. Flesh and blood." Vicki stopped walking. "Try to picture it. Believers coming together to study, soaking up the teaching, asking questions, figuring out what to do. At the same time, we help set up a supply line so people can survive."

"Would you let anyone in who wasn't a believer?"

Vicki started to answer, but Judd cut her off. "What if some say they really want to know more, but their real intent is to expose us to the Global Community? What if they want to lead them right to us?"

"We have to use caution," Vicki said. "We'd have to discern—"

"Use your power of discernment like you did with that guy Charlie?" Judd said.

Vicki threw the stale candy bar on the ground. "I cared about Charlie. He helped me carry Ryan's body."

Judd walked a few more steps. Vicki stood her ground. "Maybe it's time we split up," she said.

"That's exactly what I'm talking about," Judd said. "You're driving a wedge into the group."

"And you're the only one who can have an idea? You want women to remain silent and be good little girls. If God gives me an idea, I'm not gonna keep quiet."

"You know I've valued your input," Judd said.

Vicki scoffed. "As long as I agreed with you."

Vicki clutched the key and directions in her hand. "I'm going back for Phoenix right now!"

"Vick, that's crazy! In broad daylight?"

"Conrad said they caught Charlie with Phoenix and sent him to a shelter. I'm gonna keep my promise to Ryan, no matter what you say."

"Vick, wait!"

When Vicki reached the station she looked back and saw Judd kneeling on the ground.

Judd and Lionel waited until evening to leave Z's place. Lionel didn't ask about Vicki. Z scribbled another set of directions to the old schoolhouse and gave them to Judd.

"Sounds like you guys have been through a lot," Z said.

Judd nodded. "More than I can tell you."

Z scratched at a few scraggly hairs on his chin. He tipped his chair back. "I ain't an expert on anything but tattoos, but I do know one thing. When you got people you care about, no matter how much you fight, you got somethin'."

Z looked away. His eyes pooled with tears. "I'd give anything to spend one hour with my mom and sisters. I'd give anything to tell them about God."

When they left, Z shook Judd's hand and put an arm around Lionel. "You need anything, you holler. We could use a couple guys like you to drive for us, if you decide to help out with the supplies."

"We'll let you know," Judd said.

Lionel started his motorcycle. "I hope Pete's back when we get there."

Vicki, Darrion, and Conrad drove near the remains of New Hope Village Church. They parked their bikes behind the rubble and looked at the damage. The downed helicopter had been removed. The grass and trees were black from the scorching hail.

Vicki found shell casings from rifle fire. The bullets had been intended for her and her friends.

"From what I remember," Conrad said, "Charlie and that dog were taken to a shelter near here."

"Should we split up?" Darrion said.

"Let's stay together until we get close," Vicki said.

The three hiked to the nearest shelter. The smell of campfires and outdoor cooking made Vicki hungry. They passed tents and people in sleeping bags. Vicki motioned to Conrad and Darrion to stay back as she entered the medical tent.

A stout woman with black hair rushed about. Vicki caught her eye. "I'm looking for a friend. He has a dog with him."

"This isn't an animal hospital," the woman said.

A younger girl heard Vicki's question. She said she had seen a boy with a dog and described Phoenix perfectly. "Saw them two days ago," the girl said. "The boy seemed a little strange."

"Where'd they go?"

The girl shook her head. "A couple guys took them away in a jeep. Haven't seen them since."

Vicki thanked the girl.

"Doesn't sound good," Conrad said when Vicki returned. "The GC might have taken him in for questioning."

"Where?" Vicki said.

Conrad held up his hands. "No way, you can't—"

"They won't recognize me with the changes Z made," Vicki said. "I have to find Phoenix."

Darrion darted behind a tree. "Get down," she whispered.

Vicki and Conrad crouched low. Melinda and Felicia, the Morale Monitors, crept into the medical tent. "What could they be doing?" Vicki said.

"I don't know," Conrad said, "but if you're gonna look for Phoenix at the GC headquarters, now's the time to do it."

As Judd and Lionel reached Boyd's gas station, Shelly met them. She was frantic. "I thought you guys had left me. Pete still hasn't come back, but Taylor said he was going to find the GC and get him out."

Judd winced. First Vicki and now this. Boyd opened the garage door and let them in.

Judd heard a rumble and saw a motorcycle coming.

"Maybe that's Pete," Shelly said.

"No, it's two people," Judd said.

Mark and Mr. Stein brought the cycle in. Mr. Stein had a satchel with him.

"Did you get the money?" Judd said.

Mr. Stein nodded. Mark briefly told them about their adventure. Judd explained where Vicki and the others had gone. He looked at Boyd. "Can you point me toward the GC headquarters?"

"You can't!" Shelly said.

"I have to try," Judd said.

"Perhaps money would help," Mr. Stein said.

Judd shook his head. "Whatever's happened to Pete, I don't think any amount of money will help him now."

NINE

Phoenix

VICKI rode with Darrion. They followed Conrad to the GC headquarters in Des Plaines. Vicki was glad Commander Blancka was out of the picture, but Melinda and Felicia were not far away.

The kids parked their motorcycles two blocks from headquarters. Conrad led them to the side window. Someone was sleeping in a cell, but there was no sign of Phoenix.

Vicki walked around the corner and tripped on something metal. It clanged against the back wall. A dog barked. A door opened and a shaft of light hit the yard. Vicki gasped. Phoenix stood in a pen behind the station.

"Shut your yap!" the man yelled at Phoenix, but the dog kept barking. "This'll shut you up." The man picked up a stone. The rock bounced off the cage and Phoenix cowered.

When the door closed, Vicki rushed to Phoenix. The dog barked, then whimpered when he saw Vicki. A wave of relief spread over her. She had thought about Phoenix every day since the earthquake.

"Hey, boy, how are you?" she said gently.

Phoenix looked like he hadn't eaten in days. He wagged his tail. Vicki tried to get her hand through the fence, but the opening was too small. Phoenix tried to lick Vicki's face but couldn't.

"I'm glad to see you, too."

Conrad inspected the lock on the pen. "No way we're gonna get him out without the key."

"Why would they lock him up here?" Vicki said.

Conrad shrugged. "Maybe they're still using him to look for us."

"Wish we had some wire cutters," Darrion said.

"Let's dig him out," Vicki whispered.

The kids got on their hands and knees and scraped at the dirt. Darrion found the piece of metal Vicki had tripped over and used it to dig faster. When they had dug a few inches, Conrad sat back.

"The fence is deep," Conrad said. "We're never gonna get him out this way."

Vicki pulled at the top of the cage, but it was welded tight. Phoenix whimpered and paced, keeping his eyes on Vicki.

"We're gonna get you out of here, boy," Vicki said.

Suddenly the back door opened. Light shone in the kids' faces.

Judd and Lionel rode nearly past the small, two-story building the Global Community had seized. Lionel stayed with the bike while Judd moved closer. Judd ran toward a lighted window, peeked over the edge, and ducked when he saw someone walking toward him. He looked again. Pete sat patiently in a chair near the window.

Judd ran back to Lionel. "Pete's in there. No handcuffs, and it doesn't look like the guy is threatening him."

"Probably only a matter of time," Lionel said.

Lionel touched Judd's arm and nodded toward the building. Someone was inching up the side.

"That's Taylor!" Judd said.

Judd and Lionel rushed to him. Taylor's face was painted black.

Taylor climbed down, and the three moved away from the building.

"What are you doing?" Judd said.

Taylor took a knife from his mouth and put it in its sheath. "Jump a guard and get Pete out of there."

"You were going to kill somebody?" Lionel said.

"If I have to, yeah," Taylor said.

Judd shook his head. "No need to kill anyone. Let me try."

"I'll give you five minutes," Taylor said. "If they take him to a cell, I'm coming after him."

Judd took Lionel aside. "If Taylor leaves, alert the GC. Nobody gets killed over this."

"But—"

"Do it," Judd said.

Judd ran to the window, which was open a few inches.

The GC officer shuffled papers on his desk. "I've already told you, we believe you. The marks on the road are consistent with your story."

"Let me explain it another way," Pete said.

"I have things to do."

"Please," Pete said.

The officer's chair squeaked. "What you're saying could get you in bigger trouble than if you would have killed those guys."

"I think you're ready to hear it. If you weren't, you'd have thrown me out of here a long time ago."

"Maybe I should have," the officer said.

Judd looked through the window. Pete was leaning forward, his hands on the officer's desk.

"I don't care who you work for or what you've done in the past, God loved you enough to die for you. If you ask him to forgive you for the bad things you've done, he'll make you a new person and you can live with him forever."

The officer spoke in a low voice Judd could hardly hear. "Do you realize what my superiors would do? We're talking life and death—"

"Exactly," Pete interrupted. "What I'm talking about is life and death, too. If you reject God's way, it means you're separated from him forever."

Judd knelt. He knew Pete was bold, but he didn't know he would be this bold. He looked for Taylor but didn't see him. Lionel sat with his back to a tree.

"If I believe what you say," the officer said, "and I'm not saying I do, how would I do it?"

As Pete explained what the man should pray, Judd looked closer at Lionel. He was struggling. Judd ran and found Lionel tied and gagged.

"Taylor must have heard us," Lionel said as he gasped for air. "He grabbed me from behind." Lionel pointed to the building. "Look!"

To Judd's horror, Taylor Graham had already climbed to the second floor of the building.

"We've got to stop him!" Judd said.

Vicki rolled to her right and out of the light. Darrion and Conrad went the other way. A thin man closed the door and walked toward Phoenix. She thought they had been seen. Finally, she lifted her head.

The man held something in his hand. He opened the narrow slot and dropped it on the ground inside Phoenix's kennel. Phoenix approached warily and sniffed.

"There you go, boy," he said. "They wouldn't let me feed you. I found some scraps. Hope you like 'em."

The voice sounded familiar but Vicki couldn't place it. When he turned, Vicki whispered, "Charlie!"

Vicki rushed to him. Charlie jumped back.

"What do you want? I was just feedin' the dog. I won't do it again."

"It's okay," Vicki said. "I'm not going to hurt you."

Charlie held his arms close to his chest. *He doesn't recognize me,* Vicki thought. *Good.*

Vicki signaled for Conrad and Darrion to stay where they were. "Why do they have the dog in the cage?"

"Those guys in there are using him," Charlie said. "They're trying to find some people."

"Really?" Vicki said. "I've been looking for a dog like this. He seems nice."

"He is," Charlie said. "He's kept me company ever since my friends got killed."

"What friends?" Vicki said.

"A girl and a guy and some others," Charlie said. "They got killed by the commander before he died."

Vicki stepped closer. She wanted to talk with Charlie and tell him the truth, but she was afraid the GC officers would find them any moment.

"I have some good news," Vicki said. "Your friends aren't dead."

Charlie scrunched his face. "What?"

"Your friends are alive, and I know where they are," Vicki said. "I can take you there if you'll help me get the key to this cage."

"The guys in there'll be really mad if I do that," Charlie said. "They're looking for these two girls, and if I run off—"

"What two girls?" Vicki said.

"I can't remember their names," Charlie said. "They were with that commander guy a lot."

"Melinda and Felicia?" Vicki said.

"Yeah, yeah, that's them. They got away."

Vicki thought a moment. Why would the GC want Melinda and Felicia?

And then she knew.

"This is really important," Vicki said. "If you go in and get the key, I'll take you to your friends."

"How do I know you're telling the truth?" Charlie said.

Vicki took him by the shoulders. "Because your name's Charlie. I'm here to help you."

Charlie smiled. "How'd you know my name?"

"Will you get the key?" Vicki said.

Someone yelled for Charlie. His eyes darted to the door. "Okay."

"Don't tell anyone I'm out here," Vicki said.

"I won't," Charlie said. "You just stay here, and I'll see if I can find the key. Stay right here."

Conrad and Darrion approached as Charlie scampered off. Vicki took them to the side of the building.

"I've got a bad feeling," Vicki said. "I think the GC is trying to wipe out all the people who were involved with us."

"You think the GC killed Blancka?" Conrad said.

Vicki nodded. "And now they're after Felicia and Melinda."

"Good," Darrion said. "I hate those two."

"When they find them," Vicki said, "they'll get rid of Charlie, too."

Conrad bit his lip. "Blancka is dead. Joyce, the girl who accused you of murder, is, too. They're looking for Melinda and Felicia, and they have Charlie and Phoenix in custody. Everybody who was connected with us is winding up dead."

"Why?" Darrion said.

"Who knows," Conrad said. "Image and control are everything to the GC. If Blancka messed up, it was easier to get rid of him than give him a second chance."

"And that means they have to get rid of everybody who knew that wasn't a training exercise in that field," Vicki said, "including us."

"Just when you thought it was safe," Darrion said.

Vicki thought about the schoolhouse. They had to get Charlie away from the GC fast.

Judd watched as Taylor Graham disappeared into the second floor of the GC building. Lionel followed Judd to the front door.

"Get by the window," Judd said. "If the officer goes out, tell Pete what's up."

"Got it," Lionel said.

Judd rushed up the steps and looked inside. A man in a uniform sat at the front desk, talking on the phone. A female officer drank coffee at a desk in the rear.

Judd opened the door and calmly walked in. The man behind the front desk raised his head. Judd didn't make eye contact.

"Can I help you?" the officer said.

Judd didn't answer. He walked straight to the back hallway and closed the door.

"Hey, you can't go in there!" the man shouted. The woman put her coffee down and drew her gun.

Judd shut the door and flipped on the light. He breathed a sigh of relief when he saw the fire alarm. He pulled it. A piercing buzz filled the headquarters. Judd found a back door and rushed outside. He darted to the front and found Lionel, and the two raced to their motorcycle.

"I figured the alarm would clear the building," Judd said. "Did you talk with Pete?"

"Yeah," Lionel said. "He wants us to go on without him. I told him about Taylor. He said he'd handle it. Pete seemed to think the guy he was talking with was really close to making a decision about God."

"Let's just pray they both get out of there alive," Judd said.

TEN

The Schoolhouse

VICKI waited outside GC headquarters, peeking in the window every few seconds. Conrad and Darrion walked the motorcycles closer. Charlie finally returned with a key.

"Gotta get to my friends," Charlie said, handing the key to Vicki. "Gotta get that thing on my head. They promised me."

Conrad rolled his eyes. Vicki tried the key. It didn't work. Phoenix whined.

"I'll go back and get another one," Charlie said.

Conrad put up a hand. "We can't let him go back in there," he said.

"How are we going to get Phoenix out?" Vicki said.

Conrad ran around the building and disappeared into the darkness. A few minutes later he returned with a tire iron. "Found it in the jeep out front."

Conrad placed the tire iron at the top of the kennel door and pushed until the door bent slightly outward.

"Gonna take more than that," Darrion said.

Charlie helped. Their combined weight opened the door a few more inches. "See if you can get him," Conrad said to Vicki.

Phoenix whimpered and backed away.

"Come on," Vicki coaxed. Finally she grabbed his front paws.

Footsteps behind them.

Vicki let go of Phoenix. "You have to cover for us," she said to Charlie. Vicki and the kids scattered. Charlie stood by the door of the cage. "Cover for you," he said.

"What are you doing out here?" a man shouted.

Charlie stuttered, "Just feedin' the dog, sir."

"I thought I told you to stay inside!"

"Yes, sir," Charlie said, "but the dog was whining and hungry and I didn't think—"

"Do me a favor," the man said. "Don't think. Just do what I tell you. Come inside."

The man left. Vicki heard a voice inside the building say, "He's more trouble than he's worth. We oughta get rid of him tonight."

Vicki hurried to the cage. She took Phoenix by the paws and tried to lift him out.

"Hurry," Conrad said.

Phoenix yelped in pain as Vicki pulled his head through the small opening. Darrion tried to calm him.

"Get Charlie out of here," Vicki said.

"We're not leaving without you," Conrad said.

"They're gonna off him," Vicki said. "At least get him on a cycle so we can bolt when I get Phoenix."

Conrad led Charlie to a motorcycle, and they both climbed on.

Darrion put her arms through the cage opening and pulled at the dog's body. Phoenix yelped.

"Hey!" a man shouted. "They're stealing the dog!"

Conrad started the motorcycle. Phoenix slipped through the opening, sending Vicki and Darrion to the ground. Phoenix growled and ran toward the building. The man retreated.

Darrion and Vicki ran to the motorcycle. She tried to start it, but the engine sputtered.

Phoenix stood at the open doorway and barked.

"Go!" Vicki yelled at Conrad.

Conrad shook his head. A shot rang out.

"Phoenix!" Vicki yelled.

The motorcycle roared to life. Conrad sped off.

"Wait!" Vicki shouted. She called for Phoenix. Two men exited the doorway with guns drawn. Phoenix jumped, grabbing one man by the arm. The other man turned to get a shot at the dog, but couldn't. Phoenix bit hard and the man dropped his gun. Vicki screamed again, and this time Phoenix bounded away from the man on the ground and jumped into Vicki's lap.

Darrion gunned the engine. Vicki held on tight to Phoenix and kept her head down. When they turned into an alley, Phoenix yelped in pain and squirmed in her arms.

"It's okay, boy," she said. "You're safe now."

Darrion caught up to Conrad and Charlie. They rode without headlights through the moonlit streets. Vicki knew they had to get to the schoolhouse.

Judd and Lionel raced to Boyd's gas station. Some of Pete's gang waited for news. Judd explained what happened. Shelly said she would keep watch so Judd and Lionel could get some sleep.

Early the next morning, Judd was awakened from a deep sleep. Taylor Graham stood over him. He grabbed Judd by the collar and picked him up.

"Why did you do that?" Taylor screamed.

"Let go," Judd said.

Taylor did and Judd fell hard to the floor.

"That's enough," Pete said, grabbing Taylor by the arm.

"The GC almost caught me because of him," Taylor said.

"I told you to wait," Judd said. "Pete wasn't in any danger."

"He's right," Pete said. "Pulling that alarm kept you from doing something stupid."

"Killing people isn't the answer," Judd said.

"And talking about God is?" Taylor said. "I'm through with you people."

Taylor knocked shoulders with Pete and stalked outside. A moment later, an engine revved.

"He's got your bike!" someone said.

Pete waved a hand. "Let him go."

Mr. Stein looked at the floor as Taylor roared off. "How will I get to the Meeting of the Witnesses?"

"You'll find a way," Lionel said.

The kids moved to the office. "Where's Vicki?" Shelly said.

Judd told them about Vicki's decision to try to find Phoenix and the idea about the old schoolhouse. "She might not be coming back."

Shelly stared at him. "You're not breaking up the group, are you?"

Judd thought a moment. "We all have to make our choices," he said. "I can't stop Vicki any more than I can stop Taylor."

"But it's such a good idea," Shelly said. "We should be at the school right now."

Lionel spoke up. "Did Z give you directions?"

Judd nodded. He pulled a scrap of paper from his pocket and looked at Lionel. Something was happening. Judd felt he was losing control. Would the kids leave him behind to follow Vicki?

He handed the paper to Lionel and turned to Pete. "What about the Global Community officer?"

"Talked with him more after the fire alarm," Pete said. "He didn't pray with me, but I could tell he was close. He knows how to do it if he wants to."

Judd bit his lip. "It was pretty risky talking with him that way."

Pete sat and put his feet on Boyd's desk. "I'm not into risk. I didn't tell that guy the truth because I want to get in trouble. I could tell he was lookin'."

Judd stared at the floor.

"We've been left here for a reason," Pete said. "If people are interested, I tell them. It's as simple as that. If I read it right, the GC police have just the same chance as the rest of us."

"I'm just saying it might not be smart—"

"This isn't about smart," Pete said. "If I didn't tell that guy about God, who was going to?"

Judd looked away.

"Havin' said that," Pete continued, "I can't be sure he won't come after us. And it's a possibility Red's gang will come for revenge."

"I'm going to find Vicki," Shelly said.

"Me, too," Lionel said.

Vicki hung on tight to Phoenix as Darrion and Conrad zigzagged through the torn-up streets of Des Plaines and headed south. When they made it to what used to be I-55, she felt safer. Several times she had the feeling someone was following, but when she looked back there was no one.

Vicki gave Darrion directions as she strained to see the map Z had given. The kids rode past farmhouses and sloping fields.

"Turn here," Vicki said, seeing a dirt road leading up a hill.

Conrad and Darrion rode back and forth along the road an hour before they gave up and pulled to the side.

"Let's get some sleep," Conrad said. "We'll find it in the morning."

The kids found a grassy area a few yards off the dirt road and went to sleep. Phoenix curled up next to Vicki. When Vicki awoke, Conrad was studying the map.

"If the map is right, we gotta be really close," Conrad said.

"When do I get to see my friends?" Charlie said.

"Soon," Vicki said. "Real soon."

"What's that?" Charlie said, pointing to a brown spot on Vicki's shirt.

"It almost looks like blood."

"Phoenix!" Conrad yelled.

The dog lay still on the ground. His fur was matted with dried blood along one side. Vicki held her breath. Conrad leaned over Phoenix and inspected the wound.

Vicki couldn't look. "Is he dead?" she said.

Phoenix whimpered.

"Looks like a bullet grazed his back," Conrad said.

Vicki cradled the dog's head in her lap. Phoenix licked her hand as she petted him.

"He didn't lose that much blood," Conrad said, "but we'd better find something to disinfect the wound."

"Z said they have medicine stored at the schoolhouse," Vicki said.

While Charlie stayed with Phoenix, the kids searched for the road. A few minutes later, Darrion shouted. Vicki found her near some downed trees.

"This is why we couldn't find it last night," Darrion said, pointing to the logs. "It's blocked."

"If this is the right road, it's perfect," Conrad said. "Nobody'll find us unless they know what to look for."

Charlie carried Phoenix, and the kids walked the motorcycles around the logs. The road had shifted and would need some repair if they expected to bring truckloads of supplies to the hideout. Around a bend they found a small pond; then the road opened to a meadow. On the hillside stood the old schoolhouse. Shutters dangled, a screen door hung at a crazy angle, and the paint was peeling.

"Incredible," Vicki said.

Vicki opened the door with the key Z had given her. A long staircase leading to the second floor was just inside the door. Straight ahead was the kitchen area with a table and a few chairs. To the left and right on the first floor were classrooms.

"This is almost as big as my house!" Darrion said.

"It'd take a year just to find all the rooms," Conrad said. "There's even a bell tower upstairs." He opened a door under the stairs. His voice echoed. "There's a huge basement, too."

"Z said the bedrooms are upstairs," Vicki said.

Charlie carried Phoenix inside and put him on the floor in the kitchen. Vicki and the others searched for the supply room and found it at the north end of the house.

"What do you put on a dog who's been injured?" Vicki said, looking at the boxes of medicine. "Their skin is different from ours, isn't it?"

Vicki found a bottle of antiseptic used in hospitals. She blotted the brown liquid on Phoenix's back. The dog yelped and scampered away.

"Maybe that stuff doesn't work on an open

wound," Darrion said. "Maybe some soap and water?"

Conrad held Phoenix as Vicki and Darrion washed the wound. Vicki tried putting on a bandage, but Phoenix chewed it off.

"You told me I could see my friends," Charlie said.

Vicki pulled out a chair and asked Charlie to sit down. "Do you notice anything familiar about me?" Vicki said.

"Your voice," Charlie said.

"Who do I sound like?"

Charlie shrugged.

Vicki took the dental device off her front teeth. Charlie's eyes opened wide. "How about now?"

Charlie squinted. "I still don't know what—"

"Picture me with red hair."

Charlie screamed, "Vicki!"

ELEVEN

Danger from the Sky

JUDD walked Lionel and Shelly outside. "If I don't hear anything from you, I'll assume you made it."

Lionel shook hands with Judd. Shelly had tears in her eyes. "Why don't you come with us?"

Judd looked at the ground. "Maybe later. I'll stay with Mr. Stein. Get in touch if you need me."

When they were gone, Judd logged onto the Internet and found several messages from Pavel, his friend from New Babylon. A few minutes later he was talking with Pavel live.

"The satellite schools were set to open," Pavel said, "but the comet set them back. I'm amazed at the rebuilding, though. Carpathia has troops opening roads, airstrips, cities, trade routes, everything. And he's using each disaster for his own good."

"What do you mean?" Judd said.

"New Babylon is the capital of the world!" Pavel said. "The worse things get, the more people feel like they have to depend on the Global Community."

Judd nodded. "And you can bet Carpathia will use the next judgment for his own good if he can."

Pavel rolled his wheelchair closer to the monitor. "My father has been able to observe the potentate through his position with the Global Community. Carpathia is furious with Tsion Ben-Judah, the two witnesses, and the upcoming conference."

"From the loads of E-mails Tsion has sent me," Judd said, "Carpathia can't be too happy about the people who want to know more about Christ."

"Have you seen the exchange between Carpathia and the rabbi?"

"What exchange?"

Pavel took out a disk and sent the data to Judd. While Judd opened it, Pavel said, "My father says Nicolae has always been an intense man. Very disciplined. But now he works like a madman. He gets up early, before everyone else, and he works late into the night."

Judd read the document. It was Nicolae Carpathia's attempt to compete with Tsion Ben-Judah. His messages were short. One read, *Today I give honor to those involved in the rebuilding effort around the world. The Global Community owes a debt of gratitude for the sacrifices and tireless efforts of those who are making our world a better place.*

Another brief message encouraged readers to give their devotion to the Enigma Babylon faith. Carpathia also repeated his pledge to protect Rabbi Ben-Judah. *Those who are sincere in their beliefs should know they have the full protection of the Global Community,* Carpathia wrote. *Should Dr. Ben-Judah choose to return to his homeland, I pledge protection from the religious fanatics or others who wish to harm him.*

"Now look at how Ben-Judah responded," Pavel said.

Judd scrolled down and read the rabbi's words aloud. "Potentate Carpathia: I gratefully accept your offer of personal protection and congratulate you that this makes you an instrument of the one true, living God. He has promised to seal and protect his own during this season when we are commissioned to preach his gospel to the world. We are grateful that he has apparently chosen you as our protector and wonder how you feel about it. In the name of Jesus Christ, the Messiah and our Lord and Savior, Rabbi Tsion Ben-Judah, in exile."

"Did your dad say anything about how Carpathia reacted?" Judd said.

Pavel smiled. "The Potentate went into a frenzy. He didn't even respond to Ben-Judah's message."

Judd signed off and asked Mr. Stein to join him. "Boyd said we could fix up a little hide-out in the oil bay. One of the best ways to learn about the Bible is to help me answer people's questions."

Mr. Stein put his hands in his pockets. "My heart is in Israel with the upcoming conference," he said, "but I suppose I should learn as much as I can."

Vicki heard the sound of the engine first. She was working on a railing of the balcony when she saw two people on a motorcycle coming through the trees. She whistled the danger signal and everyone met in the kitchen. The kids had planned a strategy in case they had visitors.

When Vicki realized it was Lionel and Shelly, she let out a whoop. She ran and embraced the two.

Lionel said they had arrived late the previous night, but couldn't find the road to the school.

"Same thing happened to us," Vicki said. She gave them a tour. Lionel looked shocked when he saw the supply room. The kids had reorganized it since moving in.

"We've got a lot of ideas," Darrion said. "I want to dig an underground tunnel in case the GC ever find us." She pointed to the hillside. "It'd come out somewhere near the river."

Lionel nodded. "We need to hide a boat down there."

"The big drawback is that we don't have electricity or phone," Vicki said. "There's a fuel tank buried in the back and Conrad found a gas-powered generator, but we haven't been able to get it to work."

"Give me a shot at it," Lionel said.

When they were alone, Vicki asked Shelly about Judd.

Shelly shook her head. "He's so stubborn. I begged him to come with us, but he wouldn't."

Judd and Mr. Stein answered E-mails that poured in. People begged to know God. Mr. Stein observed how Judd answered questions

and gave advice to young people who didn't
know how to begin a relationship with God.

Mr. Stein learned quickly. He kept a list of
verses and passages of Scripture they used
frequently. Judd checked his answers to make
sure they were accurate. Soon, Mr. Stein and
Judd took shifts. While one person answered
E-mail, the other slept or got exercise.

Several weeks later, Pete returned. Judd and
Mr. Stein were thrilled. Pete told them about
finding his former gang and their reaction to
Red's death.

"Some of them wanted to kill me," Pete
said, "but most of them knew how quick-
tempered Red was. I tried to talk with them
about God again, but they wouldn't listen."

Pete turned on the television and switched
to a news channel. "You see this?"

The reporter talked about a Global
Community base that had been bombed.
"I saw something about it on the Internet,"
Judd said. "You think there are still militia
members alive?"

"The base had planes," Pete said. "They
were all destroyed. All except one. It was a
fancy six-seater the commanding officer used
to get back and forth to New Babylon."

Judd gasped. "Taylor Graham."

Pete nodded. "They're not telling everything in the report. Gotta be Graham's work."

"Can you stay with us?" Judd said.

Pete smiled. "Wish I could. Truth is, I'm not the sit-still type. A few of us are headed down south. There are a lot of people who need to know the truth."

Pete said he would leave one motorcycle for Judd and Mr. Stein to use. Judd told Pete about the boarding school and the possibility of transporting supplies to believers. Pete scribbled something on a piece of paper. "This is a truck stop where I'm headed. I know some long-haul truckers who might be interested."

"They're believers?" Judd said.

Pete smiled. "Not yet. But then, I haven't talked to 'em yet, have I?"

Pete hugged Judd and Mr. Stein. Boyd smiled at Pete. "Don't know what I'd have done if you hadn't come along."

"I can't guarantee the gang won't be back," Pete said. "I'll have a couple people check on you."

The manager thanked him. "Next time you get back here, I hope this place'll look like Zeke's station, complete with a shelter underground."

Pete had been gone an hour when the phone rang. It was Lionel.

"This is the first call we've made since we've been here," Lionel said. "Took me an hour to find a pay phone."

"How's the school?" Judd said.

"You gotta see it," Lionel said. "Z's got enough supplies for an army. It's hidden, and there are a bunch of logs across the road that leads here, so we don't have to worry about the GC. And we could sure use a computer. There's no electricity or phone, but we've been trying to fix up an old generator. No luck yet."

"How's Vick doing?" Judd said.

"Okay," Lionel said. "Darrion too. We get up in the morning and start fixing the place up. We work till sundown. Vick's started a Bible study. We take turns leading it. Wish you were here."

"Yeah," Judd said.

"How about Stein?"

Judd cupped his hand around the phone. "He's learned a lot in the past few weeks, but he's driving me crazy about going to Israel."

"Bring him here."

"I'll talk to him," Judd said. "I don't think he'll settle for less than being at Teddy Kollek Stadium. And if you guys don't have electric-

ity, I know he won't come. He'll miss
watchng the meeting."

Vicki couldn't believe the feeling of freedom.
In the time since she had become a follower
of Christ, she seemed to always be looking
over her shoulder. At Nicolae High it had
been Mrs. Jenness. At the detention center,
she had watched her back constantly. Since
the earthquake, the Global Community was
her main threat.

Now, in the peaceful setting of the boarding school, she looked forward to getting up
and going to work. The jobs were ordinary.
The kids had to take turns preparing food.
Everyone worked cleaning up the place.
Darrion's tunnel idea was put on hold. There
was simply too much essential work to be
done first.

Other than Judd, Vicki's biggest frustration
was Charlie. He pestered the kids constantly
about getting the mark on his forehead. Vicki
would explain the gospel again, but something was holding Charlie back from understanding or accepting the message.

Phoenix improved. His wound healed into
a scab, and a few weeks later Vicki could

hardly tell he had been hurt. She wondered if Phoenix missed Ryan as much as she did.

Each night Phoenix would make his rounds. He would visit each room where the kids were sleeping. Finally, he would push the door of Vicki's room open and nuzzle against her.

If only Judd were here, Vicki thought.

Judd was working on E-mails late one night, a few days before the start of the rescheduled Meeting of the Witnesses. Mr. Stein had gone to bed dejected.

Boyd burst into their downstairs hideout. "You gotta come see this!"

Judd ran to the office and saw a frantic-looking spokesman for the Global Community Aeronautics and Space Administration trying to explain yet another threat in the heavens. The news anchor asked how another comet could get by the watchful eyes of the Global Community scientists.

"I do not have an answer for that," the spokesman said, "except to say we have been on constant alert."

"Can you give us an estimate on the size and potential damage?" the spokesman said.

As the man talked, the network ran footage of the splashdown of the previous comet.

"This object is similar in size to the previous burning mountain," the spokesman said, "but it has a different makeup. This one seems to have the consistency of rotting wood."

"Wormwood!" Judd shouted.

"What?" Boyd said.

Judd grabbed a Bible and flipped to the book of Revelation. He found the reference in chapter 8.

"What does *wormwood* mean?" Boyd said.

"It's Greek," Judd said. "Tsion says it means 'bitterness.'"

The news anchor asked the GCASA spokesman, "Sir, we know now that the last comet killed a tremendous amount of fish and devastated ships on the Atlantic. What damage would this do?"

"I am told that Potentate Carpathia, along with his military and science advisors, have come up with a plan," the spokesman said. He held up an enlarged photo of a ground-to-air missile.

"They're gonna blast it from the sky," Judd said.

"If it's made of rotting wood," Boyd said, "it'll go into a million pieces."

"That's what I'm afraid of. The Bible says Wormwood will fall on a third of the rivers and on the springs of water. It'll basically poison the water supply. A lot of people are going to die because of it."

"When is the missile set to launch?" the news anchor said.

"The comet will be in range about midmorning tomorrow," the spokesman said.

"Vicki!" Judd shouted.

"What about her?" Boyd said.

"She and the others don't know about this," Judd said.

"Does this water affect believers too?" Boyd said.

"I don't know," Judd said, "but I can't take that chance. They might be drinking from a well. They have to be warned."

Mr. Stein agreed to go with Judd. After he was packed, Judd realized he didn't have directions to the boarding school. He dialed Z's place, but a message said there was trouble with the phone lines.

"We have to find Z," Judd said.

TWELVE

Wormwood

JUDD raced toward Chicago. He was mad at himself for not making a copy of the map. The sky was black. Mr. Stein pointed to an orange glow overhead. "There it is," he said. Throughout the drive the glow got gradually brighter.

Judd found a phone and called Z, but still couldn't get through. Near daybreak he and Mr. Stein pulled up to the station. The place looked deserted. Judd banged on doors and went to the back. Finally, Z's father, Zeke, let them in.

"Where's Z?"

"Couple suspicious people been hangin' around the last few days," Zeke said. "He's lyin' low."

Zeke scribbled directions on a scrap of paper. "I can't say what kind of shape the access road will be in."

"How long will it take us?" Judd said.

"A few hours."

Judd thanked him and told him about Wormwood. "I been watchin' it on TV," Zeke said, pointing to an ancient black-and-white set.

Nicolae Carpathia's face flashed on the screen, and Zeke turned up the volume.

"And I commend the members of the scientific community for coming up with this brilliant plan," Nicolae said. "Ever since the last threat from the skies, our team has been working around the clock. Their hard work has paid off.

"In less than an hour, we will launch this marvel of technology. I assure you, this burning mass of solar driftwood will be vaporized as soon as our missile reaches it. We should see little or no effect on the earth's surface."

Judd shook his head. "Don't bet on it."

Zeke handed Judd and Mr. Stein a few bottles of water. "Be prepared."

Judd and Mr. Stein roared off, going as fast as they could toward the boarding school. Judd wished he could see the launch of the missile. He was sure Carpathia would try to make as much out of it as possible. Not only could he use this to impress the world and gain followers, but the launch would also take attention away from Tsion Ben-Judah.

Judd had pulled onto I-55 when he saw a flash of light. He pulled to the side of the road and unsnapped his laptop. "I have to see this!" he said.

Moments later, Judd and Mr. Stein watched live Internet coverage of the missile's launch. As Carpathia beamed, a team of scientists showed charts and simulations of what would happen when the missile hit its target.

To everyone's amazement, the missile didn't strike Wormwood. Instead, the flaming meteor split itself into billions of pieces. The missile passed through the dust without exploding, as pieces of Wormwood wafted toward the atmosphere.

Judd shut his computer and drove on. By late morning they were dodging bits of fiery wood that landed everywhere, including waterways and reservoirs.

"Surely they will see this and know not to drink from contaminated waters," Mr. Stein said.

"I hope so."

Judd followed Zeke's directions until he came to a road blocked by logs. "This has to be it."

When he and Mr. Stein drove up, the

members of the Young Trib Force welcomed them.

Vicki was the last to emerge, her hands dirty from working on the generator. Mr. Stein hugged her. She put out a hand to Judd, then realized it was black with grease.

"It's okay," Judd said, taking her hand. "We were worried since you guys didn't have—"

"Wormwood," Vicki said. "We've been studying. Didn't you think we could handle it?"

"It's not that," Judd said.

Vicki walked away.

Judd put his computer on the kitchen table and pulled up the coverage. Video reports showed fragments of burning wood falling on Paris, London, New Babylon, Seattle, and Bangkok. Reports filtered in about those who drank the contaminated water. A reporter in South America stood near a small village. The camera panned away from him, showing scattered bodies of men and women in the road.

A panic for clean water sent people scurrying to stores. Shocked owners were dazed as hundreds of people emptied the shelves in minutes.

A grim Nicolae Carpathia faced the camera once again. This time he did not praise the work of his scientists, but called the Global Community to order.

"We must work together to overcome this terrible tragedy," Carpathia said. "I am asking the cooperation of individuals and groups. I once again must ask those who have been waiting for the conference in Israel to postpone your meeting."

"What?" Mr. Stein said.

"For the safety of attendees," Carpathia continued, "I believe it is best for all concerned to delay this important conference."

"I'd like to know what Tsion thinks about that," Vicki said.

The kids didn't have to wait long. Judd accessed the rabbi's bulletin board and within minutes saw a message. The first half spoke to Jewish believers. The other half was aimed at Carpathia himself.

The time has come, Ben-Judah wrote. *We must not waste another moment. I urge as many of the 144,000 witnesses as possible to come together in Israel next week. This will be a time of teaching, training, and encouragement we will never forget.*

Tsion then referred to Nicolae as simply *Mr. Carpathia.*

"With all the titles that guy keeps getting," Lionel said, "that has to get to him."

We will be in Jerusalem as scheduled, with or without your approval, permission, or promised protection, Tsion wrote. *The glory of the Lord will be our rear guard.*

Before dinner, Vicki approached what the kids called the reading room. Lionel had asked her to meet him there. She walked in and was surprised to see Judd.

"What are you—?" Judd said.

"Lionel asked me to come here," Vicki said.

"He asked me the same thing," Judd said.

Lionel came up behind Vicki and closed the doors. "Okay," he said, "now that I finally have you two together I wanna get a few things straight."

Vicki folded her arms. Judd leaned against a window that overlooked the balcony.

"I've taken an informal poll," Lionel said.

Judd scowled. "About what?"

"About you and Vicki," Lionel said.

Vicki said, "What happens between us—"

"Is my business," Lionel interrupted. "And it's the business of every member of this group. We're supposed to be part of the same body. We're supposed to support each other. We look to you two as our leaders."

There was a long silence. Finally, Judd said, "What did you ask the group?"

"If there was one thing you could change about the group, what would it be?"

"And?" Vicki said.

Lionel looked at the ground. "Other than getting Ryan back, we all agreed. It was to have you two working together instead of apart."

Vicki scratched her nose. Judd looked out the window.

Vicki started to speak but Judd interrupted. "That Charlie kid is on the ground out there."

"Haven't you been listening to anything Lionel said?"

"No, I mean, I think something's wrong with him," Judd said.

Phoenix barked. "What's Phoenix doing outside?" Vicki said. "We locked him up so he wouldn't drink any of the bad water."

"Well, he's out there on the ground with Charlie," Judd said.

Vicki rushed downstairs with Judd and Lionel right behind her. Charlie coughed and sputtered as he lay on the ground. He grabbed his neck.

"What happened?" Vicki said. "Did you drink from the well?"

"Only a little," Charlie said.

"I told you to leave it alone," Vicki said.

"I know," Charlie said, "I saw those girls and they asked for a drink."

"What girls?" Judd said, out of breath.

"I don't know their names," Charlie said. "I just remember 'em from back home."

"What'd they look like?" Lionel said.

"I don't know," Charlie said, coughing and sputtering harder.

"He's hallucinating," Judd said. "Get him a drink of good water."

Vicki rushed to find a bottle. Phoenix followed. Vicki locked the dog safely away. When she returned, Judd and Lionel had Charlie sitting up on the porch. Charlie drank deeply, but still seemed queasy from the well water.

"It was so sour," Charlie said. "I can't get the taste out of my mouth."

"It's lucky you didn't drink more," Judd said.

"One of the girls did," Charlie said.

Judd rolled his eyes.

Vicki kept a close eye on Charlie as they ate dinner. His face was drained of color and he said he was tired. Vicki made a bed for Charlie downstairs and Darrion volunteered to watch him.

Judd got Vicki's attention, and the two went to the balcony.

"I think Lionel's right," Judd said.

"About what?" Vicki said.

Judd sighed. "I know I've come across too

strong at times. I admit that. And I've made you feel like your ideas aren't as good as mine."

"Right," Vicki said.

"I want to be mature about this and stop fighting," Judd said. "Maybe if we got back to being friends . . ."

Vicki put her hands in her hip pockets. "I can work on that. But you can't ask me to stop coming up with ideas. God worked it out. There's somebody out there right now who needs our help. I want to be here when he or she walks through our door."

Judd nodded. "I was wrong. This place is just what we're looking for."

Vicki closed her eyes. *If he'd only said that a couple months ago we wouldn't have had to go through this.*

When she opened them again, Judd was standing over the railing, peering into the woods. "What is it?" Vicki said.

"I thought I saw somebody at the side of the house."

Judd called a meeting of the Young Trib Force that evening. Charlie wasn't much better, but at least he wasn't getting worse. Judd wondered if it had been a good idea to bring Charlie to their new safe house, but he didn't dare bring that up with Vicki and the others now. The ice was just beginning to thaw.

Judd wondered whether he could lead the kids. Would they listen to him without thinking he would boss them around?

Mr. Stein asked to say something before the meeting began. "I appreciate all you've done for me. I have been insistent on going to Israel. It has been my main goal since becoming a follower of Jesus. But it looks as if the meeting will begin next week, and I still have no way to get there."

"What about a commercial flight?" Lionel said.

"If I were able to change my identity like you have," Mr. Stein said, "I would do it. But I'm afraid it's too risky. I have enough money to buy my own plane, but I have no access to a pilot. I can only assume it is not God's will that I should go."

The kids groaned. Mr. Stein stood with his head down.

The door burst open. Judd whirled. Two girls. One had her arm over the other one's shoulder and looked pale. The other held a gun.

"Stay where you are, Stein!" the girl with the gun yelled.

Lionel glanced at Judd.

"Nobody moves," the girl screamed.

Vicki whispered something to Darrion.

The girls' clothes were in tatters, their hair out of place. They looked hungry and exhausted. But there was no mistake. These were the two surviving Morale Monitors of the Global Community, Melinda and Felicia.

"Everybody on the ground!" Melinda shouted.

ABOUT THE AUTHORS

Jerry B. Jenkins (www.jerryjenkins.com) is the writer of the Left Behind series. He is author of more than one hundred books, of which eleven have reached the *New York Times* best-seller list. Former vice president for publishing for the Moody Bible Institute of Chicago, he also served many years as editor of *Moody* magazine and is now Moody's writer-at-large.

His writing has appeared in publications as varied as *Reader's Digest, Parade,* in-flight magazines, and many Christian periodicals. He has written books in four genres: biography, marriage and family, fiction for children, and fiction for adults.

Jenkins's biographies include books with Hank Aaron, Bill Gaither, Luis Palau, Walter Payton, Orel Hershiser, Nolan Ryan, Brett Butler, and Billy Graham, among many others.

Eight of his apocalyptic novels—*Left Behind, Tribulation Force, Nicolae, Soul Harvest, Apollyon, Assassins, The Indwelling,* and *The Mark*—have appeared on the Christian Booksellers Association's best-selling fiction list and the *Publishers Weekly* religion best-seller list. *Left Behind* was nominated for Book of the Year by the Evangelical Christian Publishers Association in 1997, 1998, 1999, and 2000. *The Indwelling* was number one on the *New York Times* best-seller list for four consecutive weeks.

As a marriage and family author and speaker, Jenkins has been a frequent guest on Dr. James Dobson's *Focus on the Family* radio program.

Jerry is also the writer of the nationally syndicated sports story comic strip *Gil Thorp,* distributed to newspapers across the United States by Tribune Media Services.

Jerry and his wife, Dianna, live in Colorado.

Dr. Tim LaHaye (www.timlahaye.com), who conceived the idea of fictionalizing an account of the Rapture and the Tribulation, is a noted author, minister, and nationally recognized speaker on Bible prophecy. He is the founder of both Tim LaHaye Ministries and The Pre-Trib Research Center. Presently Dr. LaHaye speaks at many of the major Bible prophecy conferences in the U.S. and Canada, where his nine current prophecy books are very popular.

Dr. LaHaye holds a doctor of ministry degree from Western Theological Seminary and the doctor of literature degree from Liberty University. For twenty-five years he pastored one of the nation's outstanding churches in San Diego, which grew to three locations. It was during that time that he founded two accredited Christian high schools, a Christian school system of ten schools, and Christian Heritage College.

Dr. LaHaye has written over forty books, with over 30 million copies in print in thirty-three languages. He has written books on a wide variety of subjects, such as family life, temperaments, and Bible prophecy. His current fiction works, written with Jerry Jenkins—*Left Behind, Tribulation Force, Nicolae, Soul Harvest, Apollyon, Assassins, The Indwelling,* and *The Mark*—have all reached number one on the Christian best-seller charts. Other works by Dr. LaHaye are *Spirit-Controlled Temperament; How to Be Happy Though Married; Revelation Unveiled; Understanding the Last Days; Rapture under Attack; Are We Living in the End Times?;* and the youth fiction series Left Behind: The Kids.

He is the father of four grown children and grandfather of nine. Snow skiing, waterskiing, motorcycling, golfing, vacationing with family, and jogging are among his leisure activities.

The Future Is Clear

In one shocking moment, millions around the globe disappear. Those left behind face an uncertain future—especially the four kids who now find themselves alone.

Best-selling authors Jerry B. Jenkins and Tim LaHaye present the Rapture and Tribulation through the eyes of four friends—Judd, Vicki, Lionel, and Ryan. As the world falls in around them, they band together to find faith and fight the evil forces that threaten their lives.

#1: The Vanishings Four friends face Earth's last days together.

#2: Second Chance The kids search for the truth.

#3: Through the Flames The kids risk their lives.

#4: Facing the Future The kids prepare for battle.

#5: Nicolae High The Young Trib Force goes back to school.

#6: The Underground The Young Trib Force fights back.

#7: Busted! The Young Trib Force faces pressure.

#8: Death Strike The Young Trib Force faces war.

#9: The Search The struggle to survive.

#10: On the Run The Young Trib Force faces danger.